Gilt

A Lamentation's End
Novella

By Wade Lewellyn-Hughes

Gilt copyright © 2017 Wade Lewellyn
All Rights Reserved
The Lamentation's End Series copyright © 2017 Wade Lewellyn
All Rights Reserved
Published by Wisdom, Wonder, & Whimsy Books
Bozeman, Montana
ISBN-10: 0-9908175-6-3
ISBN-13: 978-0-9908175-6-7

Edited by Inspired Ink Editing
Front cover illustrated by Andrew Ryan

Published by Wisdom, Wonder, & Whimsy Books

WWWBOOKS
Wisdom, wonder, & whimsy books

Dedication

For Bryce.

Acknowledgments

As usual, I couldn't have finished this novella without my loyal beta readers. Shawn, Melanie, and Nicole, you have my sincere thanks. Also, a special thanks to Blue Falcon Editing for proving I get caught up in my own head. And, of course . . . Thanks, Mom!

The Lamentation's End Series:

Chronological order:
Tenets (novella)
Gilt (novella)
Opprobrium

Publication Release order:
Opprobrium
Tenets (novella)
Gilt (novella)

Contents

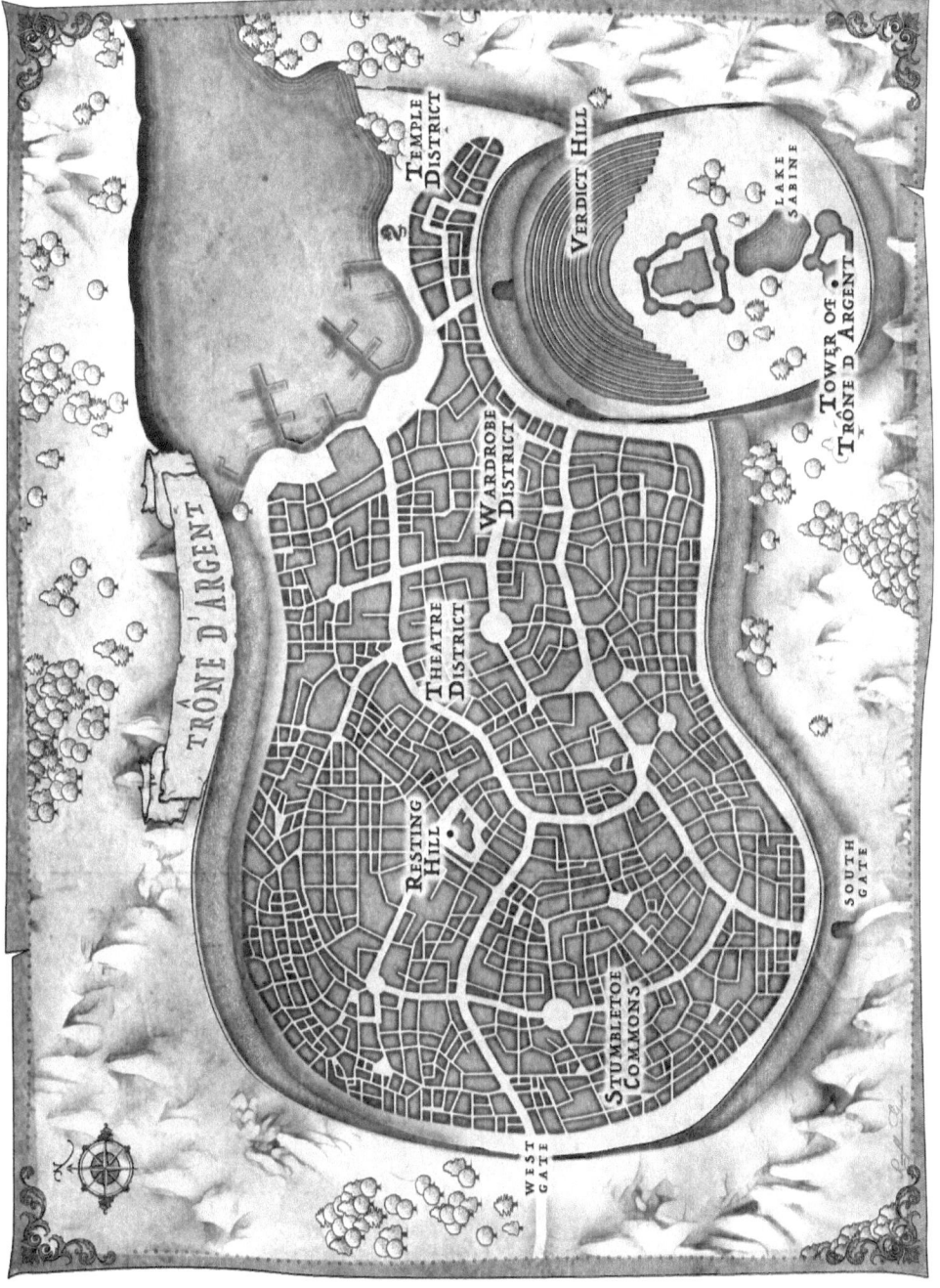

TRÔNE D'ARGENT

TEMPLE DISTRICT

VERDICT HILL

LAKE SABINE

TOWER OF TRÔNE D'ARGENT

WARDROBE DISTRICT

THEATRE DISTRICT

RESTING HILL

SOUTH GATE

STUMBLETOE COMMONS

WEST GATE

Chapter I: Shared Spirit

From between the theatre's plum curtains, Carolle spied the jewel-laden queen shifting her blue and white silks to manage a stiff perch in her private balcony. Queen Ameera's retinue of High House nobles had swathed themselves in the new pastel trend from their wigs to their hems. They ducked their plentiful chins toward their queen, spilling appreciation and excitement over each other. The queen closed her white lace fan to silence them. Showtime.

A shock of blonde hair appeared next to Carolle's face. "The queen!" Lucille squealed into her ear. "Oh, now. Don't fret, like. Queen Ameera's mam is Patevian, isn't she?"

Attempting to conjure a kinship to the queen, Carolle nodded. "A baker from Dolwyddelan." Her hand seemed strangely small and pale as she released the plush curtain, more like the thirteen-year-old girl who had joined the dance troupe than the young woman with nearly seven years of practice.

"Lucille Morgan!" Madame Davies scolded. "There're no canaries in the opening scene, good girl."

Lucille dipped her apology to their plump matron, kissed Carolle on the cheek, and fluttered out to the wings.

Madame Davies shook her tight auburn curls as she supervised Lucille's yellow-feathered doublet joining the other songbirds. The matron swept Carolle's wavy brown tresses back over her shoulders, then raised Carolle's chin higher with her knuckle. "And how's our Elysant? Ready to make Patevia proud?"

Carolle ignored the dundun in her chest and answered, "Yes, Madame." Spinning on her toes to center stage, she carried the weight of her troupe's eyes and stretched upward. Pretending to balance the stars on the nail beds of her right hand, she allowed herself one last shiver. For tonight, Carolle Ysbryd would soar and Carolle Graean would finally be laid to rest. She closed her eyes.

The metal rings suspending the curtains clinked together in a sweep away from her. Heat from the stage lamps soothed the chill on her skin. Braith's flute gently summoned Elysant, a grace slightly lifting Carolle's ribs higher. The harp and violin bound Elysant to her cheekbones. At one with the fabled milkmaid, Carolle opened her eyes.

Subtle and softly moving amid Jonjo's long horn notes, Elysant came to life in the simple farm setting. Gambion soon joined her. Within a song, the young fisherman's courting sways relayed his intent to the audience and seduced Elysant's bashful angles into bold sweeps.

Their innocent romance drew the gods' eyes. While some basked in the beauty of first love from the edges of the stage, Triumph grew envious, stricken with desire for the graceful Elysant. The god of victory aroused the manly features in Dafydd Gallivan's boyishly charming face, a darkness to match his almost-black hair and eyes. Casting his arms skyward, Triumph commanded the sun to avoid the lovers' village whenever they touched. Still their love grew through the first act.

No break had been requested between the first and second acts, so the dancers and stagehands scrambled to avoid wasting the queen's time. The curtain did not remain closed longer than a minute, maybe two, before it was swept aside.

Taking on the form of a beguilingly handsome warrior, Triumph visited Elysant's farm while Gambion rode the early-morning waves. Avoiding his advances with flitting steps, Elysant politely refused the broad-shouldered stranger and continued to offer her dairy wares.

Irate, Triumph revealed his true form by stripping a leather cap from his head and donning his crown of woven flames, or a wreath of yellow and red marigolds in Dafydd's case. His chest protruded. He commanded her betrothal to him. Prone, she bowed her head and risked declining. The god of the sun, the very god of the heavens, snapped his fingers. Withdrawing the lynchpins holding the set pieces upright, the newest members of the troupe rose in their fiery ensembles. Elysant danced her dismay away from the twirling and pirouetting flames to stage right, where she collapsed out of view, into Lucille's waiting arms.

The scene changed to the glass temple Triumph shared with his immortal siblings, giving Carolle a respite. From the wings, she stretched while Pliman, the god of the seas, comforted his brother. The gods' dance didn't end Triumph's sniveling. Pliman raised his arms. The strongest of the dance troupe dipped and rocked while carrying Gambion's simple boat out on their shoulders. Blue waves whipped their dark cloaks around Elysant's love as they spun. Finally, the waves consumed the boat and completed the act.

Again, no break had been requested from Her Majesty's balcony.

Her chest swelling with mournful ire, Carolle leaped into the woodland set, for there was but one being in the realm who could sate Elysant's fury.

Canaries, some of which were far too gleeful at having the audience of the queen, flocked around Elysant and guided her over stumps, upstage and down, and beneath the branches rushed high across the stage.

Elysant fell beneath a figure in a tattered woolen cloak. The canaries dispersed and abandoned her.

Spreading her arms, the hedge witch revealed herself. Carolle gasped. Madame Davies wore the wart-nosed mask. Carolle's reaction, a heartbeat too long, ended with Elysant's terse pleading. She channeled her anger at the error into Elysant's urgency.

Presented with a pitch-blackened knife, Elysant bowed away from the witch and hid the thin knife between her breasts. Twirling as she placed it, Carolle wished they had found a better way to conceal the cold, sticky weapon. She concluded her dance in stage center with her arms spread and her chin aimed at the sky, inviting Triumph to claim her.

Her surrender was promptly answered as Triumph danced her offstage and, as quickly as possible, back into the glass temple. His siblings celebrated their brother's victory over his mortal obsession. Only his sister Mathanas, the goddess of understanding and forgiveness, watched warily from the thrones.

Eventually, Mathanas resigned herself to the merriment on the glass floor, conveyed to the audience by the dancers' delicate steps. Triumph turned his back to welcome his sister. Elysant struck. Mathanas was faster, taking the blade in her belly to save her brother. Gently smiling at Elysant as she collapsed, the goddess brushed the back of her hand down Elysant's cheek. Triumph roared.

That was the cue for the only spell allowed in this production to be cast. A small trap door opened. Elysant fell into the arms awaiting her beneath the stage. Wearing the hood of his crimson mantle up, Mage Serrano held a small pouch against her midriff. "Fywiogi at graidd," he whispered. Specks of light spilled from the pouch and wove themselves into Carolle's clothes. On the count of three, the boys still wearing their waves flung her up through the door. She breathed a sigh of relief when her feet landed on the stage in the darkened theatre. They hadn't always been hasty enough to seal the opening fully in the past.

Green glass filtered the stage lamps, casting a verdant glow over everything except Elysant's brilliant white garb. Elysant twirled and glimmered, sentenced by Triumph to an eternity as the brightest star in the constellation of green flames thrown by the dragon Nepharni.

Gasps and cheery murmurs spurred Carolle's spinning. Permitting herself a glance, she saw the queen making her exit. The royal review would come soon in the Racinian tradition of fireworks, as it did for every new show in Trône d'Argent. Carolle forced her thoughts away from her toes and imagined the sparks of green, white, and blue her troupe prayed for. With

Queen Ameera's approval, their show would run through to spring.

The curtain closed. Carolle, still shimmering, let Elysant go with a substantial exhale. Her troupe rushed to her side.

Lucille took her hand and beamed. "There's lovely! Toss what the queen thinks."

Carolle hugged her to her side and put her other arm around Dafydd's waist.

Her line receded to the back of the stage to allow the waves, the hedge witch, and Gambion to move forward. The curtains opened. Madame Davies held the witch's mask in her hand but had changed into her finest pearl-and-aquamarine-encrusted doublet and skirt. After the first group moved to the wings, the solid line of dancing birds, gods, and Elysant toed forward and bowed.

Most of the cheers came from piks in the back of the theatre. The little people stood on their chairs and clapped their hands over their broad heads. Still seated, the human Racinians resigned themselves to tapping their fingers on their opened palms.

Before the curtain rings clattered to a close, footsteps peeled away across the stage. Canaries, peacocks, and the sea itself swarmed the stairs leading to the theatre's roof.

Carolle ran to the long hallway they had used as a costumery. She slid her sweaty, glowing garments off and let her skin breathe. A pair of blue eyes reflected her costume's spell through a scenery cart's wheels. She draped her arm over her nipples and hurled a nearby boot at the voyeur. "Get an eyeful, Brendan! You're never seeing their quality again."

The twelve-year-old son of Madame Davies bolted from his hole and down the hall, likely to the safety of his mam's skirts.

"A pervert you are!" Carolle yelled. "You draff!"

Fanning Carolle's back with her feathered arms, Lucille said, "Come now! We'll miss it!"

"All right, keep your hair on," Carolle replied. She ducked into an oversized tunic she recognized as Dafydd's, wrapped herself in the first skirt she found, and painfully raced barefoot toward the stairs, hand in hand with Lucille.

They reached the roof and the cool air of a young autumn night.

Madame Davies harrumphed at Carolle's outfit. "There's a risk! You're in the wrong nation for those, Carolle Ysbryd." Their matron glanced around as though a Racinian may have been hiding in the nervous troupe.

"Please, Madame Davies!" Lucille begged.

The hedge witch returned to Madame Davies's features, but she released them with a tired stare. They ran past her to the tittering youths at the eastern balustrade.

Falling in line, Carolle and Lucille filled in the gap next to Dafydd and drank in the moonlit view of the marble Wardrobe District. Verdict Hill rose beyond it, ringed in nine more tiers of marble, each ring of High Houses grander than the one below it. Capping the hill, the seven towers of the castle of Trône d'Argent gleamed. From where Carolle stood, the towers looked as though they could very well reach the Glades on the moon.

"Nothing?" Lucille asked Dafydd.

He shook his head. "Ych a fi," he groaned upon seeing his tunic. "You're going to wash that."

"Get Brendan to do it," Carolle said.

A whistle screamed from Verdict Hill. White sparks burst into the night sky. Then blue.

"Green, green, green, you," Carolle chanted under her breath. If no more fireworks followed, they had failed to charm the queen.

Another whistle. Exhilarated shouts erupted when the green sparks burst above the Hill to complete the colors of the Patevian flag.

Madame Davies squeezed Carolle and Dafydd against her bosom. "By month's end, Virtud Luz and Cambreoen will be begging the Patevian Royal Dance Troupe to come!" She stepped back, searching. "Why for is Serrano not by here? There's planning to do, man!"

Carolle shared a grin with her friends while they waited for Madame Davies to realize their more immediate concern, for the still-booming fireworks weren't considered the pinnacle of the queen's approval.

"Good gods," the woman uttered and balked with wide eyes. The true honor, beyond the extension of their show, was a midnight ball within the castle gardens. She screamed, "Pastels!"

Releasing a thunderous laugh, Carolle inadvertently silenced everyone. "Madame Davies, we've prepared for this."

"Yes, yes, yes, yes, yes . . ." Madame Davies panted as she turned circles to catch her thoughts. Then she raised her chin. Clapping unnecessarily to gain the troupe's attention, she commanded, "Wear only clothes I've approved. Remember your poise and your Common. Ladies, I'll permit glass jewelry tonight. Glass for Elysant and pastels for Racine, should anyone inquire. Gentlemen, I expect breeches and hose. Don't be thinking your hairy legs can escape my eye, Jonjo Williams! Let's show Racine that Patevians can be just as sophisticated, like." Scattering in a truly unsophisticated sprawl, the troupe zipped to the stairs. "No costumes!" she blared for good measure.

"Carolle. Dafydd," Madame Davies called.

Lucille frowned and continued toward the stairs with the others.

"The queen'll be wanting to grant you—us—a momentary audience." Her wringing hands bunched up her satin gloves. "To ease your nerves, I've had something special tailored for my two stars. Come with me."

At the very end of the excitement echoing up the theatre's stairs, Carolle leaned down to Dafydd's ear. "I'll bet my pudding tonight that she makes you wear the flower crown."

He returned a friendly grin. "I'll do it, if you wear the hag's dagger in your cleavage." He stood still and wrinkled his nose. "You've got pitch all over my tunic, haven't you?"

"Steady," she said, prodding him on. "I'll wash it." And she'd need to wash herself. It'd be tragic if Carolle Ysbryd had to debut covered in sweat and pitch. "May as well be Carolle Graean," she mumbled. A smile forced itself out. "The Queen of Racine, Dafydd."

"Aye. If they could see us now, eh?"

She didn't have to see his face to know the glow of success had left it. Carolle bumped him with her shoulder. "If they could, I'd say, 'Put that in your bottle and choke on it, Mam. Your no-good river rat has the approval of two queens now.'"

Chapter 2: The Midnight Garden Ball

Carolle raised her silk celadon skirt and descended the theatre's steps toward Queen Ameera's generosity. Teams of men waited to haul the boxy, silver-trimmed carriages. Over the shoulders of their ice-blue and white jerkins, they wore black wire woven into horsehead masks. Real horses were not permitted in the streets of Verdict Hill, a strange land within a strange land.

At the base of the stairs, Lucille nudged Carolle and directed her attention to Braith. The flutist in pink watched through her chin-length brown hair as the rest of the troupe scurried to claim their ride.

Madame Davies roared from within the theatre, scattering out another rush of blue and green pastel dancers. Carolle didn't see Dafydd, though she did think she saw a pair of bare legs in the mix. Gently draping her arm over Braith's shoulders, Carolle startled her. "We'll save him a seat, all right?" she said.

Braith simpered but resisted Carolle's pull to the first carriage in the line. "Oh, I shouldn't!"

Flanking Braith opposite Carolle, Lucille let out a quick, naughty giggle. "Exactly why you must." Between them, the flutist didn't have the strength to resist. They swooped her into the powder-scented carriage. Carolle checked the exit again for Dafydd. There he was. With the flower crown.

Carolle brayed and didn't care in the slightest. Howls and jeers spread through the troupe.

Dafydd adopted his best evil eye. When he reached their carriage, he said to Carolle, "Aye, all right. You win." Then he spotted Braith's meek smile inside and leaped better than he had all night. "You were magnificent, biwt!" He planted a kiss on her cheek.

She blushed and wrapped her long fingers around his hand.

Lucille patted the cushioned bench next to her and said, "Carolle, Madame Davies can ride with the troublins. No need to squeeze ourselves."

Against her better judgment, Carolle agreed. The instant she closed the door, the men drove on.

Triumph had fully left Dafydd, despite the crown. Between his boyish looks and Braith's blush gown, the pair reminded Carolle more of winsome fairies yet to find their mischief than troublins from the streets of Derw Uchel. Miscreants to performers, saved from their fates by Madame Davies and conditionally pardoned by Queen Ada.

The same as the Pixie of Bryn Mawr. Carolle rubbed the pads of her fingers with her thumb. The calluses of her bowstring had quickly given way to a dancer's delicate touch, far more quickly than her spirit had.

That was a scene far removed from Trône d'Argent's Wardrobe District. Studying the columned storage closets of the nobles, Braith said, "A real honor you've achieved, this."

"We've achieved," Dafydd corrected, resting his head against hers to take in the view.

Lucille took advantage of Dafydd's distraction and adjusted her bosom for maximum exposure. Carolle squinted at her surreptitiously. Lucille smirked back. "I've got reasons to look my best tonight."

"We've been here two days, Luce," Carolle said. "Trust you to have already found another boy to lose bloody sleep over." She tightened her squint and pinched Lucille. "Did you sneak out alone?"

Lucille swatted her hand. "Course not! Craig and Jonjo went to the market with me, didn't they?"

Carolle pursed her lips, knowing full well she'd sooner trust a dog with a down pillow than Craig and Jonjo as chaperones.

"Oh, just wait until you see my prize," Lucille added.

"He'll be there tonight?" Braith asked.

Lucille nodded with mounting excitement. A noble, then. Carolle didn't relax her patronizing eyebrow.

"You'll keep me from doing anything fun, I'm sure," Lucille teased. "Foolish, I mean."

"You're my understudy," Carolle said. "It's my job."

"It isn't, actually," Lucille replied. "Anyhow, I wouldn't trade places with you two for nothing. Queen Ameera gives me proper shivers. All steely eyes and dragon jowls. Do mind your Common. Don't want to be sounding like a real Patevian around her and that."

Dafydd sat back with a worried pout.

Carolle elbowed Lucille. "Mind our Common? We're not from so deep in the Green." She raised her chin and grinned at Lucille's teasing tongue. "Anyway, we bothered to show up on time for lessons. We've had all the preparing we need." Nevertheless, Lucille's words had started an unnatural sweat. Carolle unlatched her pale blue fan that matched the slashes in her doublet and whisked a breeze at her neck.

Giggling, Braith said, "Believe your words, Carolle Ysbryd." She intertwined her fingers with Dafydd's. "Brilliant, you both were—and will be."

Dafydd kissed her hand just as the carriage tilted uphill. It stalled until more men ran behind to push.

Braith's hair hung straight down when she leaned to gape out the window at the marble High Houses and prim gardens passing by, each ring of estates more immense than the last. She always reminded Carolle of a squire she'd seen once in a public play. Like a lath, her build did little to remove the association, though no one, aside from Braith herself, questioned how she had charmed stalwart Dafydd. The flutist's honest warmth had even coerced Carolle's secrets into her confidence.

Braith likely knew the deeds that had led each miscreant member of the troupe into Madame Davies's custody. The gods themselves could divulge acts deserving shame to Braith and be comforted by the kindest smile and patient understanding.

Once the carriage stopped at the crest of the hill, a young footman let them out. His powdered wig lowered with his bow as he stepped out of their way. Appreciating the natural autumn breeze on her collarbone, Carolle closed her fan and held it to her side in a neutral silence.

Faint strummed notes from the ball reached them on the red-bricked street. Before them stood the infamous Verdict Ring, a formidable white building encircling the grounds of the royal castle. The seat of the Racinian government reacquainted Carolle with the feeling of sneaking into a place where she didn't belong, giving her an itch around her neck, which she refused to scratch. Nobles already traipsed into the grand archway interrupting the Ring.

All agog, the troupe filed out as they arrived and waited for Madame Davies. However, upon her arrival, Gregg's lack of hose was discovered. Madame Davies shoved him into the nearest carriage and created her own scene from within.

Passing nobles eyed the ruckus curiously, though their fans remained still from gossip.

"Perhaps," Braith said, "it'd be best if you make the first impressions."

Crooking her arm in Lucille's, Carolle started the procession of the Patevian Dance Troupe. Treading through the archway, they gasped and gaped at the friezes of Racinian historical grandeur, glowing as Elysant's dress had. Delighted murmurs from ambling nobles suggested the enchantment was new and a salute to the performance, perhaps enchanted by the queen herself.

Carolle wished for a stronger breeze, strong enough to clear away the scent. She didn't mind the subtle aroma of the gentlemen's bath powders, but any three ladies smelled stronger than twenty rose gardens, filling the humid tunnel with their bouquet.

In awe at some of the more gruesome reliefs, Braith whispered to Dafydd, "How many wars began by here?"

A young redheaded lady wearing the same shade of pink as Braith scoffed and flicked her fan open fully to conceal the end of her nose and her long ceruse-caked face. The gesture relayed disgust. "Cowardly Patevians," she said in an intentionally loud whisper to her much older escort.

Braith deflated against Dafydd and let the nobles walk ahead.

Carolle scowled at the wispy red wig, for it certainly must be a wig concealing the woman's rat ears. Had they been in Patevia, the lady would have received a cowardly Patevian thrashing. But here, Carolle owed too much to Madame Davies to take it further. They all did.

Lively cheers beckoned them all closer to the merriment and music swelling in the gardens. The herald announced Lord Eccles of the Eighth Ring of High Houses and Lady Leupp of the Sixth Ring, a name Carolle would remember.

At the end of the tunnel, stairs led down to the topiary menagerie, grand fountains, and tents occupying the wagon wheel of pathways over the lawn ending at the hedged gardens nearer the royal castle. The castle's seven white spires invaded the sky like birch trees with balconies of spiraling polypore mushrooms.

Beneath a canopy, enchanted with the same spell as the friezes, Queen Ameera Koenig of Racine and her court socialized on a pavilion, a stage for all to gaze upon as they danced. The orchestra, a full orchestra, quelled their song on the far side of the pavilion, casting all attention to Carolle and her friends. Carolle donned a smile and suppressed a nervous swallow.

The herald announced them individually. Hands laden with libations and pastries applauded. Carolle didn't resist a satisfied smirk at the ovation she received, compared to Lady Leupp's. Following directly behind Dafydd, Braith's welcome, aided by the tail end of the queen's fanned encouragement, had been grander than the noble's. A spike of guilt hit Carolle when she realized Madame Davies deserved the bulk of the recognition.

Strumming back into a spirited symphony, the musicians encouraged several nobles to restart the dancing lines at the front of the pavilion.

With the queen swiftly preoccupied by her immediate company, Carolle gladly guided the others toward the puddings. She worked her way through the crowd of beckoning nobles, offering thanks and humility with a restrained tongue and a loosely held fan. Besides Lady Leupp, the nobles welcomed her with chatty hospitality. She wasn't sure how many could have truly witnessed her performance, as more milled about than the theatre could hold. Not that insincerity surprised Carolle, not from nobles. Few sins would when it came to their kind.

Emerging from the perfumed throng, Carolle realized she had lost her friends to the temptations around them: Lucille to the sugar, Braith and Dafydd to the Luzian fire dancers spewing alcohol onto candles in shocking blazes.

Coiling water dragons with their spouted streams partially blocked her view of the swinging flames. Seeking a reprieve from the pleasantries, Carolle marooned herself in the dragons' mist that had created a refreshing gap in the crowd. Golden light played across the Luzians' olive-toned faces and their white-and-red livery as the fire circled. Passion held in singular focus, they were exquisite.

Hyacinth sweetened the wet air. A petite woman with rich brown skin and shoulder-length curls braved the fountain's spit to stand between Carolle and the burbling dragons. Pale purple beads hung low in an intricate necklace over her lavender silks. The woman swallowed the missing bite from her scone, then asked in a Daijon accent, "Excusez-moi. Are you well?"

Delighted to see no fan in the stranger's hand and tickled by the heap of strawberry jam and clotted cream on the woman's scone, Carolle admitted, "What it is, I keep wondering when the joke will reveal itself. Being honored in the royal gardens of Racine? Us? Me?" A former footpad hidden in silk and camlet.

"Ah. In my travels, I have learned the best way to fight that feeling is to make friends. Shall we find solace in each other's company? Together, we can intimidate and awe with our foreign manners." The Daijon's free hand went to the beads over her chest. "I am Gbad'Wu."

A baritone rumbled, "Lady Carolle Ysbryd?" As striking as the sun, a middle-aged noble wore yellow velvet over his rotund stature at the edge of the dampness. A goldenrod ostrich feather drooped from the topaz brooch on his flat cap, likely intended to distract from his misaligned nose. The extravagant feather bobbed when he bowed and nearly took his cap with it.

Carolle hid her amusement behind her open fan until she remembered the insult it implied.

The noble maintained the small smile in his graying beard. In fact, his blue eyes held too much admiration for her. A lecher bartering for a bride?

"High Lord Rodinger Bernard," he said. A high lord? Only the nobles in the Tenth Ring, those closest to the throne, held that title. Carolle curtsied. To Gbad'Wu, he asked, "And you are Mage Kimball's friend, are you not?"

"Oui, for several years," Gbad'Wu answered. "Carolle and I were admiring the fire dancers, Lord Bernard."

"Indeed," he replied. "We find ourselves fortunate to have many talented performers in our company this evening."

Without taking her eyes from the dancers, Gbad'Wu said, "Yet I wonder how the Caperi would feel about seeing their art performed by Luzians." Barely above a whisper, she added for Carolle, "The Caperi men dance without shirts. You understand my preference." Strawberries scented the statement.

Carolle grinned.

"That's debatable," Lord Bernard said. "Is art not best shared?"

"There is sharing and there is stealing," Gbad'Wu replied. "In ten years, will Racinians believe the Caperi first danced with fire or that the Luzians always have? More importantly, do the dancers know the . . . the word? The significance of the dance? It is pretty but also spiritual. These men do not even chant during their dance."

Lord Bernard conceded with a head tilt. "Yes, I hadn't considered that."

Gbad'Wu finished her scone while they watched the performance. Carolle heard her take a deep breath. "I do not mean to stir conflict, Lord Bernard," Gbad'Wu said. "My agitation is not with you. I fear I betray my mother's ancestors by attending a celebration in the shadow of Racine's royal castle, which the Creb built for a different purpose."

"Creb?" Carolle asked, embarrassed at assuming the woman was pure Daijon, especially now that she noticed the bump at the bridge of the woman's nose. "I'd be proud if my ancestors fought Racine." Carolle's cheeks burned upon remembering the high lord's presence. His admiration vanished. "I'm only saying Patevia gave in rapidly. Now the rest of Cyr treats us like cowards. Untrustworthy, too. Our magi aren't even allowed their own Tower, mind."

Gbad'Wu's brown eyes met hers. "Perhaps. However, after their banishment to the deserts, the Creb know very little separation from the Daijon tribes. Patevia survives; your culture survives. And your lands have been restored." She raised one shoulder to shrug. "Which was wiser?"

"I feel I should remind you, Lady Ysbryd," Lord Bernard put in, "that the queen mother heralds from Patevia. Queen Ameera is half-Patevian, which is why I believe she endeavors to right the wrongs of her former empire with such passion." Gbad'Wu grinned skeptically at the high lord. "Insofar as she's able."

The Creb-Daijon conceded this time. "Elanis too has great respect for your queen. Mais, Queen Ameera cannot undo all of the empire's wrongdoings, if even those of her father."

Lord Bernard stepped into the mist and stooped conspiratorially. "This sounds like an excellent conversation to have over tea. Would you care to join me?"

Afraid her contributions would be laughable at best and wholly offensive at worst, Carolle glanced about for her troupe. Madame Davies's curls whipped from side to side behind Dafydd. They surely searched for Carolle as they approached the queen's pavilion. Carolle eased farther out of their sight, unwilling to conquer her nerves and face the queen just yet.

Around the fountain, Lucille bit into a choux pastry. Thick pink filling leaked onto her glove. She went to lick it but spotted the chiseled features of an approaching noble with a short, blond ponytail. Lucille launched the pastry over her shoulder and into the fountain.

Carolle startled those around her with a guffaw. "I'm sorry. My laugh is a whip crack, it is."

A grin crossed Gbad'Wu's lips. "A wonderful trait." Then she said to Lord Bernard, "No tea, merci. If you desire my opinions, supply another scone. With jam and cream."

The choux faux pas didn't deter Lucille's wooer, who wordlessly persuaded her into a stroll toward the hedged gardens near the castle. Before they wandered far, Carolle seized her alibi for Madame Davies and said, "I'm sorry; I must go. Pleasure it was to meet you, Gbad'Wu." She curtsied. "Lord Bernard."

"Et vous," Gbad'Wu replied. "May we meet again, ma chère."

Trailing the noble and Lucille, Carolle picked up her friend's discarded, iced gloves. The pair strolled under a white-painted metal arch identifying the Air Garden and ventured behind a stretch of hedges. Carolle skipped ahead.

Walled in by gilded bird cages, bench swings spread out among the hanging baskets of begonias in the Air Garden. The noble escorted Lucille through the gentle tones of the elegant windchimes to the swing that was farthest away and the most obscured. Content not to embarrass Lucille unless old habits resurfaced, Carolle enjoyed the sweet scent of the potent blossoms as she spied through the sleeping birds' cages.

Someone snickered behind Carolle. She straightened and tapped her finger on the metal cage, pretending to beckon a bird until her face cooled. Casually, she turned.

A lithe nobleman slightly older than she came forward from the tapered hedges of the Fire Garden. Above his wry, loose smile, a flip of brown hair defiantly held purchase. He snapped closed his golden snuff case, pawed at his nose, and stowed the case in his red jerkin, opened to his unlaced shirt and smooth chest. He brushed back the rolled cuffs of his pink shirt sleeves and peered through the cages next to her. "Do you fancy spying, Elysant?" he asked.

Carolle answered, "Oh, simply admiring the pretty birds, me." Her flush descended her neck.

A courtier bustled out of the Fire Garden's hedges. She picked a few twigs from her purple wig and brushed down the back of her skirt. Leering at the noble standing with Carolle, the courtier drifted toward the music.

The noble shrugged off Carolle's unspoken judgment. Bloody tossing nobles.

Carolle checked on the lovebirds. Lucille's suitor had slung his jerkin over the back of the bench and now lounged in his half-laced shirt. The hunt in the man's eyes suggested he saw the world in two shades. One worth taking to bed and everything else. Her mam's type of lover, hefty purse or no. Carolle rounded the cages into the Air Garden.

"Chester!" Lucille said, playfully fighting his roaming fingers. "That's twice you've compared my breasts to apples."

He offered the fruit a lion's smile.

Extending Lucille's gloves, Carolle called out, "You dropped these."

Lucille jumped and privately glowered at her.

When Chester saw the noble following Carolle, he stood. "Gaines," he said in a deep voice.

Carolle maintained her distance from the bench swing and jostled Lucille's gloves for her to retrieve them.

Lucille's face pleaded for civility. "Son of Lord Fellows of the Eighth Ring, Chester, please allow me to introduce my friend Carolle Ysbryd."

"Elysant? Gaines wanted to meet you," Chester said, lifting his opened hand toward the noble behind her.

Gaines shrugged sheepishly.

"We've met," Carolle said. "Luce, let's return now. Madame Davies'll be wondering where to we've been. We wouldn't want her finding us by here, not with what's occurring in these bushes. However quick the need." She tossed the gloves to Lucille, who roiled. A sharp jerk of Carolle's fan coaxed her off the bench.

"Agreed," Gaines said, aggravating Chester as much as Lucille. "Why are we here, Chester, when we should be enjoying the talent of these dancers in their natural habitat? Imagine the envy we could rouse."

Surrendering, Chester ducked into his jerkin. Lucille helped him lace it up. When they were nearly done, Gaines asked Carolle, "May I have the pleasure of a dance?"

"You keep those fingers to yourself, good boy." With a glance to ensure Lucille followed, Carolle walked on. "I've never been one to watch the butcher work."

Gaines flinched out a scandalized laugh and caught up. "You cut me to the quick."

"What do you want of me, Gaines?"

"It's Lord Barimor Gaines, actually."

She faced him fully to glare her lack of concern.

"Ah, never you mind. You are regarded as a lady now; you have gained the queen's admiration, after all. I merely wish to extend my congratulations with an offer of employment."

Checking behind her, Carolle found Lucille and Chester had slowed to an arm-in-arm dawdle. She tarried outside the Air Garden. "Speak clearly, man."

"Firstly," he said, gesturing to the Fire Garden, "I must apologize. Lady Peltier and I have given you a horrid first impression, a terrible way to begin an association. Secondly, while you are a lady, you have no wealth." His hands rose to placate her. "And the career of a dancer is short-lived, is it not? You are what? Twenty years old?"

Carolle didn't answer. Satisfied Chester and Lucille were close, she moved their conversation along the path to the festivities.

"How many more years could you uphold the strain of Elysant?" Gaines asked. "Ten, if you're lucky? Then what? Die in poverty?"

"Please tell me this isn't some daft marriage proposal."

Gaines chuckled. "No, no. I'm flattered, but no. You're the athletic type; my tastes run a touch—"

"Slower?"

"Healthier."

Perhaps they should have remained in the Air Garden; there were too many witnesses for her to strike him now. She consoled herself by throttling her closed fan. "Then what are you on about?"

"My proposal is this: you enter my employ while your show remains in Trône d'Argent, and I shall pay you enough to live comfortably into your dotage."

"Look, you, I'm not for sale, so take your—"

"Please!" Gaines cut in. "Maintain your discretion. I propose nothing untoward."

Lucille and Chester had taken a break in their stroll to whisper and cwtch. Carolle opened her fan and slapped it closed to gain their attention. The gesture ruffled Gaines's feathers as it drew other eyes to them. Lucille took advantage of his distraction to stick out her tongue. When the lovers moved again, Carolle said, "You're speaking through the mud. I'm not being funny, Gaines; I can't see through your desperation to hear what you're on about."

His mouth pressed closed as he thought. "It's sensitive but well worth your time."

The milling couple reached them. "Go back to the others, Luce," Carolle said. "I'll be along now in a minute."

"How about a tart or two, Apples?" Chester asked.

Lucille giggled until she caught Carolle's disgusted grimace.

Gaines allowed them a generous lead and offered his elbow to Carolle. Carolle reopened her fan and accepted. His arm was firmer than she had expected.

"Three hundred," Gaines said.

Carolle raised her eyebrows. "Three hundred gold?" He wasn't mincing words now. She would be set for years.

"Gold?" Gaines spit in insult. "What am I, a smithy? Three hundred plat."

Chills cascaded through Carolle. With that kind of coin, she could mentor her own dance troupe for troublins without royal sponsorship. There'd never be a coracle awaiting her or her friends at the end of their dance. Nevertheless, she held her expression placid. As did he.

"Gaines, what do you want?"

Chapter 3: The Dragon's Ear

"For three hundred plat," Carolle repeated, fanning herself evenly as they strolled. What would a noble believe worthy of such a payment?

"I won't palter; there are risks," Gaines finally said. "Lord Rodinger Bernard of the Tenth Ring of the High Houses. Intrigue him. Enter his confidence."

Her fan stilled. "And? That can't be all."

Glancing about again, Gaines whispered, "And . . . let's start there. Earn his trust. Prove yourself capable, and we'll discuss it further."

Carolle tugged on the crook of Gaines's arm and guided him away from a gaggle of approaching courtiers. Next to a grand fountain of seven bears with copper salmon in their maws, she released him. Shielded by the loud streams from the fish, she asked, "You want a spy? Someone to tell you he buys affection on Drell Street and cries himself to sleep in a bottle?"

Gaines's sage-green eyes lit up in amusement. "The grumpy codger holds his secrets, secrets that may bring harm to Racine. Get his defenses down. Further details will come." To Carolle's doubt, he said, "If it wasn't obvious, I'm buying your trust here."

Another pompous nobleman called out to him. Gaines waved halfheartedly and made sure the man didn't intend to interrupt them. "As I said, there are risks. Use caution. A High House lord of the Tenth Ring can have it appear anyone below the throne has absconded of their own merit, never to be heard from again."

Sobered by his vagueness, Carolle asked, "If it's dangerous, why not hire a mercenary? Not a dancer to dine by his side."

"You are new, less of a threat," Gaines answered, "and allowed lenience for uncouth behavior as the circumstance demands."

She set her jaw, though she understood his meaning.

"Besides, you have, well, a certain uniqueness that qualifies you to be the opening we've been waiting for." He pretended to button his lip. "You'll see what I mean."

"'We'?" So he did this to benefit more than himself and that foolish Chester, assuming Lucille's suitor had a mind capable of intrigue. "How many nobles need Lord Bernard's secrets?"

Gaines didn't elaborate. "Are you capable of completing this task?"

"I'm capable of trying."

The noble wrinkled his nose and raised it at her. "I shall ask again. Are you capable of completing this task?"

For all she cared, the nobles could assassinate each other, provided she had her coin and no blood on her hands. Gaines's ambiguous risks nagged her, but she would do this for more than herself. "Yes, for definite. For three hundred plat."

"Good. That's the crotchety ogre there, next to Ameera."

Under the pavilion's glowing canopy, Queen Ameera beamed at the heavyset high lord and tapped her closed fan against his arm, a sign of great affection.

"I know," Carolle said. Her pulse quickened, sensing where this was leading. She had already offended the high lord. Now she needed to restore favor and appease a queen. "He introduced himself earlier."

Elated by the news, or perhaps impressed, Gaines beamed. "Marvelous." He grabbed Carolle's hand, put it around his forearm, and pulled her along. "Fortuitous moments are fleeting."

Five steps forward, Carolle put herself on stage again. Fanning herself with an easy rhythm, she let Gaines lead her down the carpet between the circling dancers to the queen's pavilion.

Two guards stood vigil at the stairs. Both mirokar appeared human aside from the four brown twisting horns protruding from their helmets. Nobles often hired mirokar as soldiers but only if their inhuman features showed through their armor. Carolle knew better than to be intimidated, however, having played with several as a child. She felt sorry for them, being put on display to further the fear humans felt in their presence. But then, what else should she expect from bloody nobles?

Elegantly poised, Carolle adopted Braith's humble smile and delicately neared the queen's conversation. Gaines mirrored her confidence better than her humility. The spell's light worked wonders for his face, making him beguilingly pretty enough to speed Carolle's pulse.

"Your Majesty," Gaines said, "it's my pleasure to introduce—"

Queen Ameera thinned her lips at Gaines's unlaced jerkin and rolled sleeves but then smiled brightly for Carolle. "Lady Carolle Ysbryd," the queen said, "as you shall be known in Racine henceforth." Ten years easily separated Carolle and the woman with brown plaits woven through her silver crown. Pearls and opals adorned the blue silk of the queen's gown in intricate diamond patterns. "Our elegantly tormented Elysant. Have you met High Lord Rodinger Bernard of the Tenth Ring?"

Lord Bernard whipped off his hat and put it over his heart to bow this time. "I have had the honor," he said.

Carolle gracefully curtsied. "Thank you, Your Majesty. Lord Bernard, an honor again indeed."

The queen twiddled two of her gloved fingers in the air, prompting a powder-wigged servant to present her with a black lacquered box. "There is no need to state the honor, my dears. This shall more than suffice." Opening the lid, she tipped the box and reached in. A silver drop pendant dangled from the chain in her fingers. "I bestow to you, Carolle Ysbryd, the dragon's ear."

The tear-shaped pendant lit on Carolle's palm. Queen Ameera wound the dainty chain around it. "Present this to the guardians of the dragon's den in the Temple District to gain an audience with Harishnu, Trône d'Argent's water dragon. In exchange for the droplet, Harishnu offers advice on matters of great personal import. If conflict stirs your soul and you feel compelled to visit him, may his words move you as your eximious performance has moved us."

Stunned by both the gift and the thought of meeting a dragon, Carolle curtsied again without taking her eyes from the silver.

"As there are no other gentlemen about to assist Lady Ysbryd," the queen said over Gaines's head, "Rodinger, would you mind?"

Gaines quit fiddling with the lace of his left sleeve to allow Lord Bernard to pass.

Carolle raised her locks off her neck. The cold metal pendant sent chills through her when it touched her skin. With the clasp closed, Lord Bernard let Gaines resume his ignored position.

Pleased, the queen said, "I have awarded the same to your Lady Davies and Lord Gallivan. I do advise you to visit separately. Harishnu has a tendency to be forthright in an unfortunate capacity."

Lord Bernard grumbled, "Regrettably, never in matters of state."

Carolle realized they were waiting for her response. "My generosity shall always pale in comparison to yours, Your Majesty." She received a nod of approval. With an earnest grin, Carolle said, "I meant to say earlier, that is a lovely shade of yellow, Lord Bernard." At least his sleeves and hose could be considered pastel, even if his breeches and jerkin blinded eyes as well as the sun.

"Well . . ." Lord Bernard rolled his hand in the air. "It's not really within my character. But tonight, I felt compelled to have a spot of fun. You understand, to truly be seen. A whim Her Majesty has yet to voice an opinion on, thankfully." He winked, stirring guilt Carolle promptly forced down.

Queen Ameera tapped his arm with her fan again. "I admit to being torn. Risks are welcome in Racinian fashion, dear Carolle. Yet the misses take their toll." The queen's eyes trolled up Lord Bernard as her smile grew. "Perhaps it would be best if I look you solely in the eye tonight, Rodinger. We owe you that much for the yoke we have settled on your shoulders."

"Never a burden to take up Racine's call for peace, Your Grace."

With his sleeves knotted closed and his jerkin laced up to his neck, Gaines cleared his throat and piped in, "Racine is fortunate to have such a servant, Lord Bernard."

"Ah," Queen Ameera soughed. "Bumptious young Gaines. I did not see you earlier." She gave Lord Bernard a sidelong glance. "And here we were speaking of peace."

"Yes, Barimor," Lord Bernard said, rubbing his bearded chin. "What are your opinions on the rumored treaties with the Warring States?"

Smugness returned to Gaines's features as he thought on his reply. "I'm afraid my father's opinions reflect my own, my lord, Your Majesty. The Warring States would be better served under Her Majesty's rule, if not governed by the Verdict Ring directly. Racine can strengthen the States through our leadership and achieve a lasting peace." To the queen, he said, "I like to believe those opinions would have been shared by our late King Clyde, may his soul guide us from the Glades."

"Sins of the past do not skip generations, young Gaines," the queen replied. "Carolle, dear, when you come in from the cold, your cheeks shall have a healthy flush. I advise you not to waste it on little Gaines. Some mistakes need only be imagined in order for one to learn from them."

"Your Majesty?" Gaines asked with a choked laugh. "If I had my sword, I would offer it for you to finish me swiftly."

The queen's steely green eyes regarded him. "I am a mage of the great Tower of Trône d'Argent, petite Gaines. What would I do with a sword that I could not do with the very air in your lungs?"

Gaines paled and swallowed. He offered a subservient nod. His presence alone worked to their disadvantage.

So, Carolle decided to use that banter. "It pleases me to find I share your opinion, Your Majesty," she said. "I have no interest in climbing a suitor's nose to reach the stars."

A blush entered Gaines's tanned cheeks, which amused the queen greatly. Fluttering her fan, Queen Ameera delivered a "bravo" and spread the fragrance of rose petals. She then took Carolle's hand and walked her away from the orchestra to a far corner of the pavilion, wordlessly clearing out the courtiers. "If other matters behave themselves, I look forward to spending more time with your troupe over the coming months. My heart, though I am stringently Racinian, pleads to know more of my Patevian heritage."

"We'd be thrilled, Your Majesty," Carolle said. "All of us grew up with bedtime tales of Queen Tanwen's courtship to King Clyde. Baker to queen. A fantasy, that. I'm sorry to see the queen mother isn't in attendance. I do hope she is well."

The queen's gaze roamed over the spires of the castle. "Unfortunately, that is not the case, Lady Ysbryd." Her levity reappeared. "Come to an afternoon tea next week. Lord Bernard is hosting. Your presence may keep his gray demeanor at bay long enough for others to brave acceptance." The woman's grin heated Carolle's cheeks. "Bring Lady Davies as well. Her nerves may have settled enough to permit conversation by then."

Carolle dipped. "Honored, I am, Your Majesty. Diolch yn fawr."

"Croeso." The queen's fan fluttered again. "Fabulous."

Queen Ameera brought Carolle back to the noblemen, who were splitting an awkward silence. "Rodinger," the queen said, "you must invite Lady Ysbryd and Lady Davies to your tea next week. I insist."

Lord Bernard replied, "Of course, Your Majesty." He asked as the queen escorted him away, "Is it mine now?"

Gaines pinched Carolle's sleeve to get her attention and accompanied her down the stairs and off the carpet. "I'm glad you chose to be friends, Lady Ysbryd. You truly are the perfect bait."

"Charming." Her glare went unnoticed.

"I shall send you a dress for the tea with the first half of your payment in the morning. Don't be late and do maintain your discretion as you note anything of interest."

"How do I know what's of interest?" Carolle asked. "You could tell me that much, man."

Halfway to Lucille and Chester, he deliberated. "Perhaps. First and foremost, keep your focus on befriending the high lord, but—and only if it's not a risk—hone your ears for further mention of the Warring States." He lowered his chin and used his green eyes to hold her attention. "Pursue it safely. I'll temper any impatience; you deepen his trust." With that, he went on alone to interrupt Chester and Lucille's laughter.

By the water dragon fountain, Madame Davies held her side and fanned herself too forcefully. Carolle lifted two steaming cups of tea to excuse the closing of their fans and offered one to her matron.

Madame Davies took what was likely her first deep breath since meeting the queen. "Indomitable woman," she muttered, receiving her tea. "Sweet as honeyed butter to Dafydd and me one moment, devouring a gossiping courtier the next." She jiggled her legs beneath her swishing skirts with one of her loosening exercises. "But that's by the by. We've survived to shine another day; that calls for wine, not tea."

"Madame Davies . . ." Carolle winced while delivering the news. "Queen Ameera has requested we join her for an afternoon tea next week."

"I? Me? Duwiau mawr . . . When? What should? No, not to a tea, but what?" Madame Davies spluttered. She cleared her throat when some nobles wandered by, though they didn't pay them any mind. "Lucky, we are, yes?"

Carolle agreed with the truth underlying her statement and said sourly, "Racinian high society can't get enough of us." Even in a mercenary capacity. Still, a fool alone would pass up that coin. Carolle silently reprimanded herself for following her mother's dogma; anything for a penny, everything for a gold.

"Listen to me," Madame Davies said, "a gibbering wreck when I trained all of you to conduct yourselves well and that." She set her cup on the edge of the fountain. "Well, enough of this, I say. Go on, then. This is a ball, innit? We do dance and we're not leaving here without proving it."

Dragged along toward a rousing melody, Carolle's attention returned to Gaines, then to Lord Bernard's cheerful grin for the queen. Leave it to nobles to make her feel like a river rat again. Carolle Graean had survived the night after all.

Chapter 4: Tea in a High House

Lord Bernard's invitation hadn't arrived until the day prior to the tea, despite his attendance at Elysant's every dance since the first. Gaines's delivery had arrived the morning after the ball, as per his word, with a hefty embroidered purse.

Carolle paced the small bedchamber she shared with Lucille and Braith in the theatre's dormitory and reread Gaines's note. She handed the note to Lucille. "Favorite color, my arse. What's he thinking? The queen'll pretend not to see me if I wear this." She plucked at the hem of the satin canary skirt, thankfully a shade softer than Lord Bernard's yellow had been. "What kind of man can have a courtier dress sewn—and tailored—overnight?"

Lucille dropped the note on her bunk next to Braith. "The kind I do hope to know better! Chester said Barimor Gaines is in the Eighth Ring of High Houses, too."

"I envy you both," Braith said. "Not of the courtship, mind, but the fancy gowns, royal teas, games of intrigue . . ."

"One hundred and fifty plat!" Lucille squealed. She cast her admiration to the purse on Carolle's bed again.

"It hardly seems real," Braith said, "and makes practicing the flute seem very plain."

"Don't envy us, Braith," Carolle said. "Patevians meddling in High House affairs . . . I nearly refused Gaines for fear of what Madame Davies would say if she found out . . . until that purse came by here."

Lucille shot her a tired look and went to the purse. "Refused? A large price to pay to keep Ol' Davies happy." Flipping open the embroidered flap, she peeked inside. "You'd feel better if we enjoyed some extravagance for ourselves, wouldn't you? With this, we can get our own dresses proper tailored by dawn."

"You leave those coins alone, good girl," Carolle said firmly. "We're not spending a halfpenny until the job is done. I won't go having it all pulled out from under us and be beholden to a noble. You know the saying. 'If you can't see the cage for the gilt, you're already trapped.'"

Lucille shared Carolle's mam's dedication to all things shiny and hadn't heard a word.

Carolle closed the purse. "And you be careful with that Chester Fellows, Luce. I'd wager his bed cushions a lot of backsides."

"Oh, he isn't like that," Lucille said. "Chester is very considerate, like. You should see his smile, Braith. Like a heroic prince from a fairy story, he is." She practically swooned as she stared into the middle distance.

"Bollocks. He's an oily soul," Carolle said. She tempered the statement by adding, "As all nobles are. Chester may be the amethyst in the rocks, but make him prove it before he's got you wearing a wooden nose."

Holding up the dress to block Lucille's scowl, Carolle studied the white bustier. Daffodils and Patevian poppies in thread of gold accentuated the bust. The same pattern lined the underside of its double sleeves, a nod to Patevian fashion. "How long has Gaines been planning this?"

Lucille reached under Carolle's pillow and removed the silver drop necklace. "You could ask the dragon for whatever Gaines is after."

"No, Luce," Braith said. "He'd know it was for profit."

"Fine," Lucille replied. "Then you can ask him about Chester." She giggled at Carolle's glower.

Laying the dress as flat as she could manage on her small bed, Carolle said, "I meant what I said, Lucille Morgan." She took the necklace, wound it up in her fist, and placed it back under her pillow. "Now, come on, then. There's only one thing for it. Help me get into this sunbeam."

Once the final ribbon had been tied and the abundant mother-of-pearl buttons had been looped, Carolle couldn't deny a sense of power, contrary to the color. "You're probably right," she said, admiring the fit in the mirror. "I shouldn't worry about catching Lord Bernard's eye." They laughed.

Carolle gripped Lucille's wrist and spoke to herself in the mirror. "I'm just the tool, a well-paid tool. I'll do the job. And we'll enjoy the coin."

"We certainly will!" Lucille agreed. Bolstered by the excitement in Braith's eyes, Carolle resigned herself with as deep a breath as she could pull.

Someone knocked on the door, three firm raps. Brushing down the back of Carolle's skirts, Braith murmured sweet worries. When Lucille had hidden away the purse, Braith let Madame Davies enter in her pistachio-colored ensemble, awash in her newly acquired lavender scent. Boldly chosen, the ruffled bonnet actually worked well with the matron's auburn curls and pale complexion.

"Duwiau mawr," Madame Davies uttered, taking in the yellow snugness. She pursed her lips.

"A gift," Carolle said.

Snatching their matron's wrist, Lucille spun the woman to face her. "Please, Madame Davies! Carolle's got a real chance! Promise you won't interfere!"

"What's this now? A chance at what?" Madame Davies asked Carolle.

"I won't lie to you; she's got a proper suitor!" Lucille lied. "A lord of the High Houses, like! Do let them get their moment alone, if it comes to that."

Madame Davies huffed. "Alone?"

Leave it to Lucille to take it a step too far. "Steady, Luce," Carolle said. "You'll draw the fairies' ears and have it doomed before it begins." Madame Davies's shoulders went rigid and Carolle explained, "There may have been a passing interest and an inquiry made. That's all. Luce is getting far ahead of the rest of us."

"He sent you a dress to wear for him!" Lucille said.

"And this is wanted attention?" Madame Davies asked.

The care in the question stirred Carolle's guilt. Yet the good would outweigh her lie. She timidly nodded.

"The High Houses are no guarantee for happiness, Carolle Ysbryd. You'll think clearer on it in the spring. After Elysant's time here, yes?" Carolle would have given a plat to hear Madame Davies's true thoughts and another to assuage them.

Fluttering her pistachio-green fan, Madame Davies asked, "Have you got a fan to go with that dress?"

Carolle's fan splayed its golden flowers for her matron's approval.

As they left, Lucille said, "Do be careful."

"Careful?" Madame Davies barked down the corridor. "We're going to tea, good girl, not a riot! The queen may chew us up and spit us out, but she won't be beheading us, like."

All the same, Braith and Lucille accompanied them to the street.

The early-afternoon sun heated the inside of their man-hauled carriage trundling toward Verdict Hill. Carolle unlatched a window. Children in simple linens chased after them. Carolle waved back until the guarded gate to Verdict Hill blocked their cheerful escort.

When the carriage tilted back in its uphill climb, Carolle daydreamed about how she'd use the plat first. Buy a permanent home? Or begin a troupe for troubled young ones? She frowned out the window. The very concept of Madame Davies's generosity was as foreign to the occupants of these marble High Houses as she was.

Madame Davies teased her with a cooing sound. "You do like this noble boy. A bat could see your nerves, girl. You don't have to be an oracle to see what's occurring there."

Playing it off in good humor, Carolle shook her head.

"Don't you worry. I won't be interfering, if his interests won't be interfering with our show. I'm not ready for Lucille Morgan to be Elysant— and neither is she."

When they came to a stop, Madame Davies closed her eyes and rolled her shoulders. "Bright eyes. Bright smiles. Poise."

Carolle followed her matron out onto the red-bricked broad street. Flowering lobelias, as vibrant as the marble estate's royal-blue doors, decorated the powerful High House in tiered baskets. Full hedges lined the austere white walls, a welcoming contrast to the stark Verdict Ring behind her. Carolle grinned at the gentle touches, not at all what she expected from the curmudgeon everyone claimed Lord Bernard to be.

However, the welcome didn't extend to the doorman's face. The wrinkled servant stooped. "This way, if it pleases you. Her Majesty, Queen Ameera of Racine, and High Lord Bernard of the Tenth Ring shall be delighted by your presence."

Indigo paint coated the estate's hallways above the dark oak wainscoting. Portraits, tapestries, and overstuffed settees filled the long gallery with a sense of hospitality. Somewhat worn hospitality, but warm all the same. Yet guards in dragon-emblazoned armor lurked at every corner.

Midway down a wide staircase, they drifted left and came to an archway. In the daylight on the other side, Queen Ameera mingled with courtiers. Carolle stepped through when the herald received her name. Her jaw dropped. She had seen smaller banquet halls than this High House balcony.

Carolle hadn't taken in the full view of the snow-covered peaks beyond the bay before Madame Davies hauled her away by an arm around her waist. She hadn't even heard her name announced. Thankfully, neither had the queen over her courtiers' discussions of the lace-worked fans spreading up the wall of Lord Bernard's home to form a multicolored rose.

"Do Racinians do anything small?" Carolle asked Madame Davies. Musicians piped and strummed their way through Anstef Myranna's "Great Suite" while more nobles judged tapestries, poetry, and paintings set in opposite corners of the balcony. Informal judging ran rampant when their conversations lulled. "Tea? It's a pastel and silver eisteddfod, this." Sadly, not a body danced.

Carolle saw neither Lord Bernard nor Gaines. If Lord Bernard wasn't in attendance at his own tea, how was she supposed to befriend him? Sneak into his residence?

Surrendering to Madame Davies's urging, she entered the savory aroma of pasties and plentiful morsels. A bit overwhelmed, Carolle clung to the end of one of the tables on which plates of sugared apples formed a spiral between whole pumpkins and gourds. Madame Davies helped herself.

Spotting a familiar face, Carolle shared a relieved smile with Gbad'Wu. In contrast to the Racinians' stiff skirts, cornflower-blue silks flowed about Gbad'Wu's legs as she made her way over with a full plate. Her lilac Daijon necklace had been replaced by a nearly identical blue one. "At last, two foreigners who are not entangled in the rivalry of the Towers," she said.

"Towers?" Carolle asked. "I haven't seen any mages, bar the queen."

Gbad'Wu raised a canapé with thick orange purée and pointed her pinky to the far end of the balcony. "They are arguing over the alchemy contests around the corner." She took a bite.

"Gods," Carolle gasped. "It's even bigger?" Perhaps that was where Lord Bernard hid.

While Carolle scanned the far end of the balcony, a silver-mantled mage with her hood down broke through the crowd. Uncommonly short, the mage's black hair had been pinned into a bump on her head. Gbad'Wu waved the woman over. Her spectacles rose with a friendly grin. "Alchemy proves as fruitful as ever," the mage said. "Bless them. They are ever so proud of their continued failures. Alas, alchemy remains as useless as those frilly fans." Thumbing over to the large rose, she glanced down at the fan Carolle held. "No offense intended."

"None found," Carolle said. "I forget it's there half of the time." She caught Lady Leupp making a face in her direction and lowered her voice. "And fight the temptation to use it as a weapon the other half." Madame Davies cleared her throat at that comment.

The voices around them receded as rose petal perfume wafted forward. "I find offense," Queen Ameera said with a playful flourish of her fan at the mage. She lifted the mage's black bell sleeve and cocked an eyebrow. In tiny letters, PASTELS repeated in pink, blue, and green embroidery across the velvet. "Elanis lost her say on etiquette when she became a mercenary and forgot the function of fashion."

"For the Hook, Ameera," Elanis replied, jerking her sleeve free. Carolle went cold, but the queen curled the corners of her mouth in amusement at the mage's curt response. "You make it sound like I'm some fopdoodle thug. I'm wearing a skirt. What more do you want?"

The queen's eyes lit up with a retort, though she didn't voice it. Red to her ears, Elanis's bespectacled glare said she didn't have to.

"The only way back into my good graces, Mage Kimball," Queen Ameera said loudly, "is to help in judging those useless, frilly fans these ladies have spent so many hours creating." The queen's jovial demeanor relayed her lightheartedness to the noblewomen around them.

Elanis groaned with her mouth closed.

A copper-skinned man in a sapphire mantle from the Alabonian Tower knelt before the queen, blocking her return to the fans. "Your Majesty, it is my pleasure to deliver King Casdar of Alabon's well wishes."

"How kind," the queen said in an amiable tone. "Please see them returned." She fanned for the four ladies to follow her around the mage, who wasn't sure if his king had just been insulted. Neither was Carolle.

Carolle scanned the corner of the balcony for Lord Bernard again but, trapped in the queen's pull, trailed along to the crafted rose.

Out of the Alabonian mage's earshot, Elanis snorted. "He sends mages as messengers now. Does he mean to appeal to the mage under your crown?"

A low hum from the queen relayed her agreement. "Of course he does, El. Nothing else has rewarded his efforts. I give the king some credit for trying new tactics."

Drawing them closer beneath the handmade fans, Queen Ameera elaborated. "To the blissful masses, marriage is a natural solution for two single monarchs. No one believes a queen's agenda to reach further."

"Well, that—" Madame Davies bit her tongue too late.

"Speak freely, Lady Davies," the queen said. "I do enjoy hearing my mother's accent on your tongue."

Fluttering her fan a little too fast, Madame Davies continued, "Well, I just meant to say that sounds like it would be a prosperous union, Your Majesty. Alabon is a lovely nation, by all account." She shrugged to dismiss her statements.

The queen put her finger to the red lace edging the fan hung before her and tightened a loose thread. "While the nation is wealthy and the largest border Racine shares, make no mistake; the very nature of marriage to a king grants sparse advantage to me, far less than it places in his hands. In fact, it robs me of power. If that were not deterrent enough, King Casdar is forty years my senior. One need not assume his main purpose in marriage shall be producing an heir." She visibly shuddered and mischievously grinned at their blushes.

Elanis folded her arms and thinned her lips, making Carolle wonder if the mage's relationship with the queen surpassed friendship.

Queen Ameera flicked her fingers in the Alabonian mage's direction as though trying to rid herself of a mosquito. "Pests. When I need a man to govern Racine, I shall make my own through a more enjoyable endeavor."

Allowing herself a guarded smirk, Carolle glanced to the balcony's corner again. She needed to free herself, but how could she without insulting the queen? Carolle asked, "Will Your Majesty be judging the alchemy contest as well?"

Elanis snorted. "Yes, Ameera, doesn't Grand Diviner Sylvester appreciate your input?"

The queen pursed her lips at the gibe and tapped the mage's arm with her fan. "A misstep I shall own. Inviting the visiting mages to this tea was meant to instill a sense of community, to accrete the Towers for once. Alas," she said, tipping her head in the messenger's direction, "they have their own agendas."

As the queen deepened her explanation for Madame Davies, Carolle sensed her opportunity for escape and took a step back. Gbad'Wu noticed. "I'm famished," Carolle mouthed.

Gbad'Wu's amused face called her a liar. She put her arm through Carolle's to hold her in place. When Queen Ameera finished her sentence, Gbad'Wu bit into a puff pastry and moaned. "Carolle, ma chère, you must try a vol-au-vent. They are divine."

"Yes," Queen Ameera said, "please do. The salmon canapés are my favorite. A local delicacy we export to Patevia."

With the queen's attention back on Madame Davies, Carolle silently thanked Gbad'Wu. Vol-au-vents and salmon canapés secured, she skirted the long way around Queen Ameera's view. In doing so, she caught sight of Gaines. He briskly scowled and pointed his chin to the balcony's corner, as though she hadn't figured that out.

Fewer nobles milled about between the silver, amber, sapphire, and crimson mantles. Proudly toiling with fizzing concoctions and chiming metalworks, the mages from all four Towers bantered with varying degrees of civility. The Tower of Trône d'Argent's grand diviner, a spindly man in robes as white as his hair, intently listened to explanations of a clockwork snail.

A barn owl on Grand Diviner Sylvester's shoulder twisted its head about to watch Carolle pass by in her quest for Lord Bernard. There he was, in muted grays and blues, sitting alone at a small table with his attention spearing a book.

Carolle approached, though Lord Bernard didn't notice, turning over a page and twiddling the graying hairs on his chin. She hated to bother him but had three hundred reasons to do so. "The view is beautiful, Lord Bernard," she said. "Your home is lovely and all!"

Breaking free of the page, Lord Bernard closed the tome. His belly laughs at the yellow of her dress scented the air with sweet pipe grass. "A Patevian ally in more ways than one!" He rose into a stiff stance.

"I'm sorry to interrupt your reading." Carolle read aloud, "The Miltiad Manifesto?"

His face grew stern. "Yes. When you're in my position, it's of dire importance to stay abreast of our neighbors' laws, no matter how inimical and fatalistic."

"Miltiad is one of the Warring States, innit?"

"Quite right," he answered. His bushy eyebrows lowered over his deep-set slate eyes. Perhaps she shouldn't have asked that. The silence lingered into awkwardness.

"I wanted to thank you, Lord Bernard," Carolle said.

"Oh, you're welcome," he replied. "The queen insisted, after all."

"Yes," Carolle said. "For the invitation. But also, I wanted to thank you for attending our show. I've seen you in the audience." The man blushed and turned his focus to the gibing mages. "Real grateful, I am, to have your support."

He met her eyes long enough to nod once.

Carolle placed her fan over her heart in a show of sincerity, tickling her collarbone with the laced edge. He nodded again. Gods, was the man thick? Her mind began grasping for polite conversation, a topic of mutual interest. What did nobles talk about?

A young woman sang out, "Lord Bernard!" Lady Leupp swept over and offered her hand to him. Her eyebrows twitched upward in surprise at seeing Carolle there. The lady put her back to her. "There you are. I thought I might find you back here in need of suitable company." She giggled like a loon, but the fan behind her back drooped in insult.

Next to sick of the excessive perfumes these nobles used, Carolle would have encouraged Lady Leupp to use more.

"Not at all, Ludmilla," Lord Bernard replied. "Lady Ysbryd has saved me from my solitude."

Ignoring the mention of Carolle, Lady Leupp said, "You have not replied to my invitation, my lord. The fête is in two days."

"Fête?" he asked.

Lady Leupp poked her fingernail at him playfully. "You know! At Lake Sabine. I do one every year now." Her fingers walked up his sleeve to his shoulder.

"Ah! Of course," Lord Bernard said, flinching away. "Thackeray mentioned something of the sort. Yes, well, you know . . ."

Carolle sensed her opportunity, though her mouth soured before releasing the impertinent words. "Lake Sabine? I hear it's exquisite this time of year. I do love a good view, I do."

"Oh, yes," Lady Leupp replied, still trying to ignore her. "The leaves began to turn last week."

"They must be inspiringly brilliant by now," Lord Bernard said.

Carolle imitated a doe-eyed girl, silently begging him to show her. His blank gaze lingered on her.

Partially turning her head Carolle's way, Lady Leupp added, "Of course, you wouldn't be able to see them yourself. The lake lies between the royal castle and the Tower of Trône d'Argent. Access is unfortunately restricted to those who belong on Verdict Hill."

Lord Bernard's eye twitched. "As a matter of fact, yes! Yes, Ludmilla, I shall be there, and Lady Ysbryd shall be my guest."

"Will she?" Lady Leupp replied in a high voice.

Carolle curtsied to hide her victorious smirk. "You honor me, Lord Bernard. Lady Leupp. I can't wait to see it!"

"Now, now," Lady Leupp said. "I understand your excitement, but let's maintain our decorum. Shall I let the help know to prepare that simple, simple speckled bread your kind are so fond of?"

Beaming in spite, Carolle lost her interest in deference. She let her fan dangle, feigning ignorance to the returned insult. "Oh, a nice offer, that, Lady Leupp, but no need to bother. They'll likely over spice it, as your kind are so fond of doing." Carolle stared at the woman's excessive use of cosmetics and picked up a salmon canapé from her plate. She offered it. "But Queen Ameera is right; this salmon is delicious. Have you tried it?"

Declining with a raised hand, Ludmilla Leupp bade Lord Bernard a good afternoon. The lady's face drooped with poorly veiled disdain for Carolle as she headed off to the nobler side of the balcony.

Lord Bernard's face smoothed when Carolle peered up at him, but she could have sworn he had been smirking. "Well, that seems serendipitous," he said. "It remains to be seen, however, if your reward will be worth the price."

"Oh," Carolle moaned. "It's my reward alone, innit? I am ever so grateful to you for enduring the fête on my behalf." With sincere gratitude, Carolle dipped. "Please allow me to leave you to your reading, Lord Bernard. Thank you again for your invitation to the fête. I look forward to conversing with you more then."

On her way back to Madame Davies, Carolle's nerves led her to devoured her plate of nibbles and go back to the tables for more. Gaines loitered about nearby and worked his way over as she helped herself to more of the smoky salmon. "That was quick," he said. "I trust you've secured another invitation."

"I have," Carolle answered, debating between the mysterious orange purée and the green one. "You may be interested in knowing he's reading The Miltiad Manifesto as we speak."

"Miltiad?" Gaines asked. "Hmph. When do you see him next?"

She chose the orange. "I'll be his guest to Lady Leupp's fête."

Gaines groaned.

Carolle retracted her hand from the vol-au-vents and looked at him.

"What's wrong?"

"Nothing," he answered. "You did well." Yet he sneered at the foie gras. "This simply means I must accept Lady Leupp's invitation myself."

Carolle shrieked a laugh and startled him away from her. He rounded the table and examined the selections on the opposite side.

"I don't need supervision," she said quietly. "I'm capable of enjoying a fête on my own."

"No," he said. "I mean to come along as a distraction for Lady Leupp. She cannot resist an unwed man who can help her climb the Hill. I'm only an Eighth Ring lord, but I like to think I'm more enticing than the stodgy fool of a high lord you'll preoccupy."

"Very nice," Carolle remarked. "You leak charm, you."

Pinching a soft croissant from a napkin-lined tray, he asked, "Do you own a dress he hasn't seen?"

Carolle answered in annoyance, "Yes, I've got one."

"One?"

"Pale blue, very pretty if I do say so."

Gaines snickered and tore into his croissant. "I'll have it seen to. Please continue to impress me, Lady Ysbryd."

With that, Carolle made her way back to the queen's circle, which still included Madame Davies, fanning herself to winnow away the red from her cheeks.

Chapter 5: Gossip and Games

In the aft tunnel through the Verdict Ring, Carolle and Lord Bernard didn't rush to remedy their tardiness for Lady Leupp's fête. Their dawdling steps echoed amid the friezes detailing the Tower of Trône d'Argent's history. Lord Bernard tucked his slender leather case under his arm as he delayed them further to relay the story behind each relief. Impressively knowledgeable and so pleased to share, the high lord piqued Carolle's interest. But her true prize awaited at the end of the tunnel.

Carolle paused. Wintergreen trees and snow coated the peaks above mirror-still Lake Sabine, encircled in trees enchanted by autumn's brilliant spell. On a shorter hill opposite the lake, the Tower of Trône d'Argent took her a moment to recognize, for it wasn't a tower at all.

"Tower by function," Lord Bernard explained when she inquired about the stately, columned palace. Colonnades arced out on either side of the Tower, supporting a line of statues over the manicured trees and sprawling lawns. "The magi ascend as they progress through the curriculum to receive the highest honor, their mantle. Not a clever metaphor, but I suppose children need to understand it."

Unable to keep her eyes on the stairs, Carolle nearly stumbled a few times while descending to the valley where Lady Leupp's pastel tents offended in a garish line along the gold-and-red autumn foliage. Lord Bernard offered his arm.

Carolle traipsed at his side into the sweet scent of cooking fires and onto a knoll where Lady Leupp's guests bowled downhill. Farther down the lawn, Gaines aimed to seduce everyone in his green ensemble's well-fitted jerkin. He spared Carolle a secret smirk before devoting his charm to consoling Lady Leupp, whose throw had missed all nine pins.

Lord Bernard exchanged a few pleasantries with the nobles on the knoll and explained their tardiness. "Forgot the pieces," he said, lifting his dusty leather case for them to see. Then, without introduction, he carried on walking before Carolle had even withdrawn her hand from his arm.

Instead of invading the jovial attendants near Lady Leupp, Lord Bernard nonchalantly took the brick path encircling the lake. After some silver-mantled mages passed them by, Carolle whispered, "Won't someone find it rude, us sneaking off?"

"Have you not heard? My reputation carries a certain expectation. If it rubs off on you, please accept my apologies." The High House noble winked at her. "Would I be wrong in suspecting your concern for offending Ludmilla Leupp is as shallow as my own?"

Carolle rewarded him with a tight, mischievous smile.

They abandoned the trail and rustled and crunched fallen leaves on their way to an amber-and-crimson copse near the lakeside. Under a dark purple plum tree, an old scroll-worked table and benches occupied a nook open to the shore. As Lord Bernard brushed leaves from one of the benches, he said, "Insidious woman. Ludmilla seeks a husband, above all. I do not fault her determination in ascending the Rings but question her judgment when pursuing old fools like me. I could be her father, if not her grand. Transparent desperation—her sheer precipitous nature—speaks ill of her diplomatic agility. As a lord or lady achieves higher ranking, thus, too, does their political responsibility grow." He flicked the last leaf off and gestured for Carolle to have a seat.

"Ta," Carolle said. She sat, wondering what the high lord must think of her attention. Friendship, then. She breathed a little easier, relieved to be able to distance herself further from her mam's occupation, and absorbed the view of the Tower across the lake.

A swipe of Rodinger's hand across the leaves on the table revealed a checkered game board. He set his leather case next to it.

"Are we going to have our own game, then?" Carolle asked.

"Yes." With that familiar and previously misinterpreted twinkle in his eye, he unclasped his case and began arranging brass and pewter figurines on the board. "You'll learn more from this than the insincerities they volley at the fête." He gave her fan a sidelong glance. "And you won't be needing that."

As he arranged the last few pieces, he said, "I find conversation flows easier when a game distracts the mind."

Recognizing the horse, Carolle tapped its metal ears with the pad of her finger and asked, "Chess? I'm afraid I never learnt to play."

"Excellent! No bad habits to break, then." He set the empty case next to him on his bench. "You'll recognize chess's similarities to your performances. Each piece has a specified movement. Combine the movements strategically to execute the show with a favorable outcome."

Doubtful, Carolle smiled a preemptive apology.

"I frame it this way," Lord Bernard said, "so you understand the importance of the whole match and refrain from acting on willy-nilly reactions to what appears correct in the moment."

By naming the pieces after characters in Elysant on the Glass, Carolle quickly picked up the movement patterns. The stratagems Lord Bernard issued challenged her relentlessly. As they played, she asked him about life on Verdict Hill, which required extra prodding to get more than grunts of apathy for social events. The one thing she knew for certain, Lord Bernard selected his friends as strategically as he played chess—and just as often.

All the while, Elysant failed to protect Gambion, her king, three times, but Carolle set her mind to slaying Triumph.

While Lord Bernard thought over his next move, Carolle enjoyed the aura of autumn and the shiny mantles passing under the colorful leaves on the path across Lake Sabine, above and below in the reflection. At least one mantle from each of the four Towers passed within a span of minutes. "Will they ever open new Towers?" she asked. "I know I'm repeating myself, but Patevia could use one. It'd be nice not to ship our magi out to Trône d'Argent or Aontus, mind."

"Yes," Lord Bernard answered, to her surprise. "Well, if all goes to plan. Naturally, that hinges on a peaceful unity floating just outside of our grasp." His thick fingers slid the bronze queen, Mathanas, to a square that trapped Gambion and prevented rescue from Elysant. "Checkmate." He opened his leather case and began clearing the board.

"We can't stop now," Carolle said. "I just learnt how to properly use the canaries."

"Pawns." He chuckled. "If you prefer it, we could continue later. As time allows."

"I'd enjoy that," Carolle said, relinquishing the pieces she'd intended to hold captive until securing another engagement with him.

Lord Bernard closed the case and rose. "I'm delighted to play against a fresh mind, though I must admit a slight offense at championing the petty god." His laugh lines deepened. "Well, I have an appointment with the queen and the high lords in chambers this evening and much more to do beforehand."

Strolling back with Lord Bernard's arm warming her hand, Carolle relished the serenity of her surroundings. Aside from the nobles shouting and guffawing for attention, the lake offered tranquility, something she hadn't really felt since her days as a footpad. The Pixie of Bryn Mawr had menaced traveling merchants for only two years before getting scooped up and assigned to rehabilitation in Queen Ada's dance troupe, but Carolle had grown fond of the countryside.

At the edge of the fête, Lord Bernard slowed their walk and asked, "Shall I leave you to the fête or escort you back to the Verdict Ring?"

Carolle shifted behind Lord Bernard to block her eyeline to Lady Leupp on the knoll. "If I'm already in the valley, is it illegal, like, to stay for a while longer on my own? Have an afternoon stroll?"

He, too, spied Lady Leupp's way. "Go on. My presence does not increase the worthiness of your character in accordance to this stricture or any other. I'll mention it to the royal guards. If anyone dares to raise issue against it, I shall personally pardon you." Unbending his arm, he set her free. "Thackeray shall arrange our game for the next day free of your performance. Would you prefer to play here again?"

"Yes!" Carolle answered with more glee than she'd intended. She curtsied. "I had a wonderful time, I did, diolch yn fawr. Fresh air and bright leaves. Those mountains. Can't think of a better way to spend the day, really."

Straight-backed with an air of belonging should someone try to stop her, Carolle parted ways with Lord Bernard and doubled back to the copse. She meandered at the shore, watching the reflection of the mountains and the shimmery mantles across the water.

Snapping branches brought her attention back to the copse. In unlaced green, Gaines emerged from the trees near the plum. He carried two maple goblets rimmed with silver. "You should be careful out here alone," he said. "A crazed magus may sneak up on you."

"I was feeling all right until you came creeping, good boy," Carolle replied, moving closer to speak without being overheard.

"It's that time of year again," he said, offering her a goblet. "Warm spiced wine?"

Carolle accepted her drink. She sipped the clove-and-cinnamon-scented wine, her eyelids closing halfway. Too much spice overpowered the sweetness. "Finished giving Ludmilla Leupp a chase around the lawn?"

"She's finished with me," he said, hopping up to stand on the chessboard. "For now, anyway. Lord Eccles has arrived. To Ludmilla, he presents a more promising offer. More likely to die in his sleep on the wedding night, you see."

"Ah," Carolle said. "No accounting for taste, then."

Gaines dropped to dangle his legs over the side of the table and grinned at her like a fool. "I'm sorry. Was that a compliment, Lady Ysbryd?"

Curling her lip, Carolle said, "Perhaps. But I meant it as an insult for her."

"Oh, you wait and see; we'll be friends before you know it." He fiddled with his cambric sleeves and began rolling them up. "Now please tell me you've secured your next meeting with Lord Bernard."

She swirled her wine in the hefty goblet as she paced around the table. "Aye, didn't even have to try really. He's going to teach me to play chess."

Tucking in the last roll of his sleeve, Gaines furrowed his brow. "Chess? That's a bit storybook, isn't it? The noble teaching the, um, less cultured to be sophisticated?"

"No," Carolle answered flatly. "We enjoyed ourselves today without one condescension between us. Try to imagine what that's like." She let Gaines off the hook when he bowed his head in apology. "You may want to know he mentioned there'll be more Towers 'if all goes to plan.'"

"More?" Gaines repeated with disgust. "Why? They barely keep the peace between the ones they have." He cracked the knuckles on his right hand and shook it out. "Well, no one would permit a Tower in the Warring States. In any event, as I've said, you don't need to concern yourself with those kinds of questions yet."

"I didn't ask him for you, man," Carolle said. She flittered her fingers at him. "Go on back to Lady Leupp already, lest you lure her by here."

Gaines threw a rude gesture in the direction of the fête. "Oh, as you wish." He picked up his goblet and dropped off the table. At the tree line, he dallied. "Your troupe is attending the Winter Peak gala, yes?"

"How'd you know that?" Carolle asked. "The invitation only came this morning."

He tapped his finger to his temple. "It's tradition for one of the shows to perform at the opening. Yours is the newest."

Gaines's pink lips turned downward. "Keep bonding with the codger over your lessons. We'll move things forward after the Winter Peak gala. In five weeks, we'll be bolder." He thought for a moment, drumming his fingers on his goblet. "I meant what I said; I need you to be my friend, Lady Ysbryd. Carolle." He waited for her reaction. She granted permission to use her given name by silence alone. "I shall guard your back but may need you to guard mine as well."

His statement put an itch between her shoulder blades, a guilty itch. Carolle agreed and choked down another sip of the bitter wine. "Off with you, Gaines. You bloody nobles are dramatic beyond, you are."

"As the lady wishes," he said with full bow and scrape, goblet to heart. He walked into the woods and called back, "Your dress for the gala shall be the best yet."

She smiled before she caught herself and grumbled her way back to the shore. Whatever Gaines schemed, she knew one thing for certain: the Pixie was keeping her goblet.

Chapter 6: An Evening in Peach

Five weeks flew past in a whirl of performances, practices, and chess. Winter browned autumn for another cycle, summoning the Winter Peak holiday and the most formal Racinian engagement.

Carolle assumed her place on the side of the royal ballroom's dance floor. She watched the queen's dais out of the corner of her eye, where Queen Ameera sat on her silver dragon-winged throne. Around her, the high lords and ladies of the Tenth Ring had donned their ice-blue loyal-to-the-throne ensembles. Carolle grinned at Lord Bernard, standing there dutifully in his damask coat without an inkling of joy in his features.

Trône d'Argent mages and the grand diviner filed in to stand before the queen. They dipped and bowed before turning to watch the opening ceremony. Queen Ameera raised her hand. On cue, a harp roused the musicians.

Carolle glided across the white dwarven crystal tiles of the dance floor toward Dafydd. Her arm lifted out from the rabbit fur lining her taffeta peach cape. Without touching Dafydd's fingers, she circled him and deftly avoided the hooves of the sculpture suspended in the air.

Looming above the affair, ice captured the Koenig royal crest in a life-sized rendering. The crimson dragon's wings spanned the ballroom in a frozen flight amid a snow enchantment that never reached the dance floor. Claws dangled a great elk stag by its antlers, hanging low, as though someone might miss the magical masterpiece if it didn't pose a hazard.

Four rotations of partners brought Carolle to the middle of the song and near the end of the twirling line. Madame Davies and Mage Serrano spurred the noble spectators to join in. Mage Serrano's crimson mantle jarred a bit with the pastels around the room. He swaggered around Madame Davies, who appeared quite enthralled herself, elegantly coifed in gifts from Queen Ameera, including her Racinian-blue dress.

Carolle peeled away from the line in a final twirl and entered the spectators, thankful the snowy spell chilled the air and reduced the potency of the floral perfumes wafting about. Her numbed fingers begged her for a hot cup of tea. Treat in both hands, she let her digits thaw and made her way to the petite woman in lavender silks examining the display of hors d'oeuvres. Gbad'Wu's bare arms made Carolle shudder. "It gives me the creed, seeing you in no sleeves! Aren't you cold?" Carolle asked.

Flashing a friendly smile, Gbad'Wu answered, "Not for many years. The cold invigorates my kind. A benefit of our order."

"Order?"

"My monastery, the Mount of Ukresti."

Carolle stopped blowing across her tea. "Wait, Gbad'Wu. You're a monk?"

"And a midwife," Gbad'Wu said. "I recruit lost souls to join the Mount."

"Well," Carolle said, searching for her words. She took a substantial pull from her tea, flavored with honey and lemon. "Didn't expect a monk to be wearing pretty silks and jewelry, is all. Not seen many, to be fair. Spellbreakers, really."

"More separates me from them than my clothes."

Someone tugged on Carolle's sleeve. Lucille offered an apology to Gbad'Wu for interrupting. "Have you seen, Chester?" When Carolle shook her head, Lucille went on the hunt again.

A quick scan of the room didn't reveal Gaines yet, either. Her stomach didn't mind his absence, as it had been turning against her all day with the threat of his plan moving forward. While she remained committed to the task, she had to admit she'd grown fond of Lord Bernard.

Carolle emptied her drink and gave her cup to a passing servant. Fanning for Gbad'Wu to join her, Carolle asked, "Do monks dance, Gbad'Wu?"

"Bien sûr," Gbad'Wu answered. "Yet how can I go?" She waved her arms out over the food. Then she gestured with her open hand to the table at the end of the row. "Do you see what this table offers?" The monk hauled Carolle along by the wrist. Gbad'Wu's brown scarred hands picked up a plate, added a truffled bun, and drizzled it with a buttery yellow sauce. She forced the plate on Carolle.

Amusing the monk, Carolle bit into the bun and dropped her plate on the table. This time she seized the monk's wrist to drag her onto the dance floor but turned and collided with Grand Diviner Sylvester. Choking on her bite, Carolle coughed and waved her apology. The sharp angles of his face grew harder. His barn owl stared. In control of her breathing again, Carolle said, "I beg your pardon." She curtsied.

The thin old mage asked, "Omelet is fascinated with you. Why?"

Carolle met the owl's large black eyes. "I don't know. He's cute. Aren't you, biwt?"

"She," the grand diviner corrected. He studied Carolle closely, hair to hem. Too closely. Carolle smelled faint smoke on the mage's robes.

She stepped back into the table, convinced his frigid scrutiny could see her darkest secrets: her deal with Gaines, her thieving, her mam's whoring, all of it. "Grand Diviner, have you met my friend, Gbad'Wu?"

The mage walked on. His owl's head turned back to Carolle as they disappeared into the socializing nobles.

Gbad'Wu clicked her tongue. "He treats everyone this way. In his mind, the queen herself wears the stole of a pupil."

"He has less patience for high lords," Lord Bernard said behind Carolle. "Trust me on that." He offered Carolle a delicate glass flute of sparkling wine as Elanis did the same for Gbad'Wu. "Hold on to this for the queen's announcement."

Elanis put her hand up for emphasis. "No one has the right to complain more about that man's carping than a mage raised under his reign in the Tower. I welcome you all to feel sorry for me."

"He remembers your name," Gbad'Wu said. "I remain 'monk.'"

"It's far worse when he knows your name," replied Elanis.

Turning to Lord Bernard, Carolle asked, "Where to are you hiding this time? I don't see a book under your arm."

He wagged his finger in the air. "Speaking of reading, were you able to start The Jeweler's Delight?"

"I did, as it goes," Carolle answered. "Finished it last night. Had a good cry, me. I don't know how dragons would feel being painted in that light, mind."

Carolle tapped her fan against Rodinger's arm. She hadn't intended to do so. The man glanced down at the gesture, which implied a friendship beyond formality. Surely, it wasn't too soon or too assuming. Gods, she hoped it wasn't. "Ah, yes," he said. "The story was my daughter's favorite, Carolle."

Her shoulders relaxed. "You've got a daughter? You hadn't said."

"Rodinger!" groused a balding man with more lift in his chin than his heels. Gold rings shimmered on his fingers as he prodded Lord Bernard's belly with his pipe stem. "Rodinger, talk sense into her! This shall ruin us! Make us weak against Virtud Luz!"

Lord Bernard stared down his crooked nose at the man and replied,

"I shall do no such thing, Winslow. I quite simply could not be arsed to do so."

Leaving the lords to their argument, Carolle inserted herself into Elanis and Gbad'Wu's conversation about extending the monk's stay in Racine. It stalled when Madame Davies arrived with one of the wine flutes now being served around the ballroom.

Elanis said, "Lady Davies, if you've finished your dance, the queen has requested your company."

The look on the matron's face said it all as she ogled the flute in her hand.

"There's to be a toast soon," Gbad'Wu warned too late.

Gaping at her half-empty glass in horror, Madame Davies gasped, "Oh no!"

Swapping their glasses, Carolle told her, "Don't worry. I'll set it right."

Wetting her lips, Madame Davies held the glass flute over her heart and hesitated. Carolle's fingers gave her a slight nudge, prompting the plump woman to float over to the dais and dip deeply before the queen.

On her way to the closest servant, Carolle spotted Lucille dancing with Chester. Gaines, however, remained absent. Carolle said to the server, "Afraid I had a spill, I did."

A snort caught her ear. Lady Leupp wore a new blush cape over her old blush gown in a ring of purple people. Just the sight of the woman made Carolle's mouth sour. "Clumsy after all," Lady Leupp said loudly. "Stands to reason. Even a witless dog can perform some tricks." The women giggled and encouraged her with fluttering fans. More titters and a few passing remarks followed. The second "Patevian" and the first "bitch" baited Carolle.

With fresh bubbly in hand, Carolle faced the women. "I'll defer to your expertise, Lady Leupp," Carolle said, sizing up the others. "You appear to enjoy the company of dogs." One fan fluttered, though the others hid the women's noses in blatant offense. Lady Leupp squinted a threat.

Carolle returned to Gbad'Wu's side and clinked her glass to hers.

"You play their game boldly," Gbad'Wu said.

"Don't encourage me," Carolle said. "I'll go back and punch her just to see if I can hear her bony arse hit the floor through all of those skirts." She laughed it off. "Ah, no. Madame Davies has instructed me well enough to refrain. A treasure, she is."

With a harshly shouted syllable, Lord Bernard shocked the shorter lord into silence. Lord Bernard pressed the gawking man back, freeing the space between himself and Carolle. "I urge you to desist and regain your civility," he said, maintaining his warning scowl. "Lord Winslow Gaines of the Eighth Ring, may I introduce Lady Carolle Ysbryd? I believe she is already acquainted with your son." The itch of a man barely glanced her way. "Lady Ysbryd is the doyen of the Patevian Royal Dance Troupe that has received high praise for their performance of Elysant on the Glass."

"Ah, yes. Fine," Lord Gaines said. If he knew of his son's endeavors, the man gave nothing away.

Three pops jolted everyone and saved Carolle from a false pleasantry. Silver sparkles sizzled and fell around Grand Diviner Sylvester on the dais. The mage and his owl lowered their limbs in unison. Stepping aside, the grand diviner gave Queen Ameera the floor. Clearly realizing they were now the only three on the dais, Madame Davies froze next to the throne, clenching her glass so hard Carolle feared it might break. The grand diviner flanked the silver dragon wings opposite the matron.

Armored in a silver collar suspending chains of pearls and enameled pink roses, Queen Ameera vised a closed scroll. "My loving people," she began, "on this special evening, I hold in my hands a gift to you, the very concord of our future, the seed from which our salvation shall grow.

"For hundreds of years, Racine has diligently guarded against Merith's return. A cause corrupted by many leaders in our past. An excuse to swell Racine's prosperity on the backs of conquered subjects and their lands. Let it be a source of great humility for us all, including my opponents at this gala, the men you hear muttering 'harridan,' opponents of my decision to end the empire."

The audience murmured more than one slur. Carolle's troupe had begun to cluster about the ballroom. Their independence had arrived with the civil war and the dissolution of the Racinian Empire five years ago. Gbad'Wu put her arm around Carolle.

Queen Ameera spoke over her subjects. "Victory over ignorance in our short-lived civil war raised us higher in the eyes of nations across Cyr. Racine is the grand sword, the ingenious mage, and the debonair bard. Alas, the mightiest warrior on the battlefield does not embody the spirit of accord we now require. Racine must learn also to be the generous merchant, the wise consul, and the august tower shield.

"We approach a precipice," Queen Ameera proclaimed. "False histories and entitlements have drawn lines in blood across this continent for nearly seven hundred years. Those petty wars distracted us from a true threat. I speak not of Merith's resurgence, but the Cloud over the Saratial Sea, fingering deeper into the land each day to feed on towns before it recedes." Gasps and fans stirred. "Oh, yes. The rumors are real. This evil is real. Contented ignorance has blinded us. Imperiled us. Far too long have we denied the existence of these tribulations, dismissed them as problems facing other nations.

"Racinian pride claims an invulnerability to the rest of Cyr's woes. No more. May those pompous prevarications never again tarnish your silver tongues. Racine requires allies. We require trust. We require faith to see us through the approaching days."

Dissenting voices rose loudly enough for Carolle to start making out words. Many blamed the Patevian queen mother. Carolle felt faint. Paler by the second, Madame Davies appeared as though she literally would.

Queen Ameera's jowls lifted, silencing her subjects. "The comparisons between my father's decree and my own are inevitable. Yet I assure you, my faithful, my loving people, we shall vanquish the dark forces biding their time behind the Cloud just as assuredly as we shall bury those who stand against us in salted, unmarked graves.

"Your queen's heart yearns for solidarity. We have gorged on war. We have relished in our enviable wealth. Now we must champion change. Let the lowlanders of Lekelith hear our humble call to amity. Let the

Dragoneers' descendants in Patevia and the tribes of Frysta Avfall raise their voices." Queen Ameera looked back fondly at Madame Davies, who sank into a curtsy. Carolle subtly fanned the sweat on her brow. "And yes, let the Luzians know Racine shall aid them in their darkest days."

Grumbling must have reached Queen Ameera's ears again; she cut her hand through the air. In reclaimed silence, she opened the scroll and turned the inked document to her audience. "Thirty-three nations occupy this grand continent and the Gallaic Sea. Your queen joins King Casdar of Alabon, Queen Ada of Patevia, and King Javier and Queen Valentia of Virtud Luz in extending an invitation to the countries of free men to join in the Bonded Nations. At Racine's request, Taus and the friendly Caperi occupying the Sliver in Virtud Luz shall also be offered a seat at this communal table. A table of considerable power—yes, to judge our actions and to determine consequences—but also to bring a unified force against our true foes. Humans, piks, mirokar . . . the brave must stand together, for we must supplant our shared evils with open hearts and minds."

Queen Ameera exchanged the scroll for a flute of wine. She raised her glass their way. "While Alabon and Virtud Luz recruit, our High Lord Bernard shall lend his savoir faire to Racine's call in the Archipelago and the Warring States."

Lord Gaines's grimace shouted betrayal at his superior.

"Unified, we shall triumph!" she concluded.

The queen sipped, watching the crowd as they drank or refused in silence. Madame Davies emptied her glass in one toss. The Tenth Ring lords and ladies, the magi, and those Carolle assumed to represent Racine's parishes closest to the Cloud applauded with fervor. Queen Ameera retreated from the gala entirely. Elanis followed closely on her heels. Gbad'Wu rubbed Carolle's back, whispered an apology, and trailed after Elanis.

Where was Gaines? Was this what he had been trying to prevent?

Grand Diviner Sylvester took center stage. Madame Davies stood stupefied on the dais until the grand diviner urged her down with a glare. Murmured discontent and exaggerated gasps drowned out the swelling of the music. Carolle wanted to go to her matron, but Lord Gaines blocked her path.

"You defend her against me," Lord Gaines said up to Lord Bernard. "First, she takes the military out of our hands and forces a civil war. Then she reduces the first five rings to courtiers, thanes, and delegates to the bumpkins. Now this! Explain the benefit of sharing diplomatic decisions with the Archipelago and the Warring States. The queen mother's agenda at work! And the Caperi? A barbarous people who are no better than invaders?"

Carolle ground her teeth. She hated Patevia being lumped in with the other islands, as though only together in "the Archipelago" were they significant enough for worldly matters. Lekelith alone had defeated Racine, had it not?

She flinched when Lord Gaines stabbed a stubby finger her way and said, "Certainly even a Patevian can understand her child queen is not ready to make strategic decisions of this magnitude!" If he were waiting for agreement, he got none from Carolle. "Rodinger, reducing Racine's influence further is foolishness. Idealistic nonsense!"

Looming gravely over the man, Lord Bernard warned, "Careful, Winslow. Your preference for parsimony when defending the races speaks ill of your character. In any event, your expostulation is futile; you have run out of time to convince me otherwise."

Lord Gaines reddened and scoffed. "We should be tightening our control over the Warring States! Those high-and-mighty Luzians may sway these other Bonded Nations to defy Racine outright. Due to the queen's hesitation to wed, our enemies in the Alabonian population rival the lowlanders of Lekelith. Combining the two . . ." He tightened his hands into fists. "Disastrous."

Carolle's pulse thundered. "There's cowardly," she said, surprised to hear the words slip past her lips.

Lord Gaines huffed through his nostrils.

"How much of the gold in your purse came from Patevia's hills while we suffered centuries of your rule, Lord Winslow Gaines of the Eighth Ring? Enough to buy us a seat in the Bonded Nations, not that we need Racine's permission anymore."

Lord Bernard gave her a satisfied tip of his head.

Lord Gaines barked to the nearby nobles, "Idealistic. Naive. Racine was once your empire too, young lady. Can your queen even speak Common?"

Carolle raised her fan in insult and stepped forward to stand over him. She nearly grinned when the man stepped back. "You'd have to hunt high and deep in the Green for one who couldn't after Racine's influence, good boy. Grubby miser, you are. Selfish!"

"Carolle Ysbryd!" Madame Davies scolded. Red splotches brightened her cheeks. Her nostrils flared, promising a week of regret to come.

Carolle took a step back and lowered her fan.

Shaking his head, Lord Gaines grumbled, "I may appear coldhearted to you, but I doubt you'd sacrifice Patevia's standing for Racine's sake. I cannot be shamed for protecting the interests of my family and my country." His voice thundered when he addressed Lord Bernard. "Your adulation betrays Racine, Rodinger. We shall speak of this in chambers, where the company is less diluted. We've endured enough Patevian influence around here."

A splayed fan cut off the noble's curt exit. Lady Leupp beamed an oblivious, toothy smile. "My Lord Gaines, I had hoped to see your son tonight. Has he fallen ill?"

"No," Lord Gaines answered. "Merely better served hearing of these puerile declamations from the servants. Witnessing them firsthand necessitates too much restraint."

Lady Leupp's false laugh spoiled the air with garlic. "Please let young Lord Gaines know I am eager to enjoy his company on the dance floor soon."

Lord Gaines brushed by her.

Ignoring Carolle, the tall trout dipped for Lord Bernard. "Ludmilla," he said.

Carolle watched her go and fanned herself evenly while opting for an old-fashioned, blatant sneer. Would someone not marry that woman to spare the rest of them?

Lord Bernard put his hand to Carolle's back and chuckled. "My dear, when the dance no longer fills your purse, you could give mongoosing a try. In fact, if I may, I encourage you to begin now; for if you seek to strangle every snake in Trône d'Argent, you shall accomplish little else in life."

His jest didn't soothe Madame Davies's temper. Carolle hung her head. "My apologies, my lord, Madame Davies. I fear I'm not good company this evening. The world changes on this hill; I'm meant to view it from afar."

"Poppywash!" Lord Bernard said. "I am thankful for your words, Carolle. And admire your Madame Davies all the more for her tutelage." That dampened her matron's temper a smidgen; at least it relaxed her nostrils. "We lords move borders, when we are fortunate. You move hearts almost nightly. Which do you think changes men's minds faster?" Not waiting for an answer, he asked Madame Davies, "May I have a moment alone with your ward?"

Confused, and likely concluding Lord Bernard had been Carolle's wooing lord, Madame Davies hesitantly bowed her head. "Of course, my lord," she answered. Her scowl relayed the promise Carolle hadn't been saved from her punishment. Madame Davies strode off toward the circulating bubbly, leaving them relatively alone.

Lord Bernard whispered, "I find myself with the freedom to share a secret. Will you do me the honor of being the first to learn of it? I feel I owe you for getting caught in my argument."

Carolle's mind buzzed with insults she wished had come to her in Lord Gaines's presence, forcing her to provide a rote response. "It would be my pleasure, Lord Bernard."

"Oh, now," he said, placing her hand on his forearm and patting it, "if that rapacious runt with iron in his soul can call me Rodinger, you certainly can."

Her cheeks burned when she recalled she had already established an informal friendship. She ducked her head appreciatively.

"Good," he said. "Meet me in front of Popplewell's warehouse on the docks the morning after next. No fans. No frills. No pretenses. Pure, forthright Rodinger. Pure, forthright Carolle."

Comforted by his gentle nature, Carolle consented with an idea to take their minds off her disgraceful behavior. "On one condition. Dance with me."

Rodinger spluttered and paled.

"Gbad'Wu left. Blame her, but don't burden me with finding someone else."

Worse than Madame Davies, he hemmed and hawed.

Gods, Madame Davies. The matron made no pretenses herself, watching them from across the room, hawk eyed. Carolle needed to douse that flame first. "Please give me just one moment," she said.

"Of course," Rodinger agreed. "Go on, now. Move men's hearts. And do remember, if I'm not here when you return, you're purer than half of these besotted, deceptive souls. Present company included."

She playfully gusted him with her fan. "You do wish for me to meet you on the docks?"

Defeated, he slumped like a grouch and acquiesced.

As Carolle made her way to Madame Davies' pending harangue, her stomach turned against her. The more her mind worked, the less she believed herself to be on the right end of whatever Gaines was sharpening. The young lord had better supply some clear answers soon. Otherwise, she didn't think she could continue under his employment. Not for Lord Gaines's benefit. Not for Lord Gaines's coin.

Where was he?

Chapter 7: A Grander View

"Calm down, will you?" Carolle whispered. "I said I'm doing it, Luce!" They crept downstairs to the theatre's exit to the alley. "I just want you to know where the coin comes from is all."

"Good; I'm going with you," Lucille replied, revealing the kitchen knife she had stuck up her sleeve. "What? I'm not letting you go on your own. You wouldn't let me." Lucille threw open the door. Early morning fog dampened the air outside.

Concerned, Braith stood in the doorway. "You sure you don't need me?"

"Oh, Braith bach," Carolle said. "We do need you. Here. If Lucille isn't back in time for practice, tell Madame Davies you can't find her."

Lucille pouted curtly and tugged on Carolle's cloak.

"Actually, tell her the same for me."

Hauled along by Lucille, Carolle waved back to Braith. Deserted beneath the mauve sky, Theatre Row offered itself fully to the Patevians. Carolle's plain blue woolen dress and brown cloak conjured a rush of defiance and freedom amid the columned facades. She giggled as loudly as Lucille as they raced toward Port Way.

A baker paired samples of freshly baked gingerbread with his directions to Popplewell's warehouse in the west port. Misremembering a left for a right put them in the Temple District, in front of the water dragon's den running down to the shore. White marble, like all of the buildings this close to Verdict Hill, the den sported a dome over its rectangular columned base. Alternating bands of lapis and azurite led up to a patinaed copper top. Carolle and Lucille lingered in reverence, wondering why a dragon, even a wingless water dragon, needed ten fully armored guards, until a costermonger opened his cart.

The street merchant steered them west, but not before Lucille coaxed him out of a salty pretzel and Carolle liberated a snippet of grapes. Sharing the nibbles, they chewed and enjoyed their stroll along the bay.

Fishermen and seagulls called out across the water in the light of dawn. "If this works out," Carolle said, "I want a home with this view. Those gorgeous mountains. The water and all."

Twirling a lock of blonde hair between her fingers, Lucille shot her a puzzled glance. "You never went to Trawsfynydd back home?"

Carolle shook her head.

"I grew up with a view like that."

"Did not! Liar!" Carolle teased, though Lucille insisted with fervent nods. "Mountains with snow like that? Year round?"

Lucille flung her hair back over her shoulder and admitted, "Well, maybe just in winter." The silence grew heavier as Lucille wore her thoughts on her brow. Finally, she said, "Diolch, for that night with Chester. In the gardens."

Carolle put her arm around her.

They walked like that until Lucille pointed across the water. "Look over by there. He said Popplewell's is the big one, didn't he?" Ashlar buildings edged the western end of the bay, but one rose to five stories. After ambling to prolong their exploration of Trône d'Argent, they still arrived at the warehouse early.

Braced to argue for Lucille to go back before the ruffians sobered up, Carolle pulled her into an alleyway across the bustling street from Popplewell's. A dockworker caught her attention as he searched about for onlookers near the warehouse's barn doors. Carolle and Lucille ducked behind a few disused barrels and spied. The brawny dockworker knocked. Opened a sliver, the barn doors let the man squeeze through. They resealed immediately. Within minutes, six men repeated the ritual. "What are they doing in there?" Carolle asked.

A loud clack from down the alley startled them upright. Two planks fell from a stack propped against the building. Peering into the darkness, Carolle took Lucille's hand. Her eyes adjusted to the shadows and made out a form crouching by the fallen lumber. A cloak? From beneath its gray hood, a pale mask watched them back. Carolle went cold to her core. The man dashed away from them, trailing his cloak down the alley.

They did the same, running straight into the bustling street. Carolle crossed between high-wheeled carts and accidentally cut in front of a steed hauling a farmer's bounty. The turnip-faced farmer cracked his whip over her head and shouted obscenities at them. She leaped to get out of the street and well out of the range of his whip. His vexation led to bellowed, rude remarks a fair distance farther, drawing more attention.

"Gods, who was that?" Lucille asked, holding her knife pointed at the alley.

"I don't know—put that away!"

"Shaddup!" a vagrant man yelled from the walkway before pulling up his blanket. Clearly, his patience had not recovered from drinking his way to the bottom of a barrel. Whiskey, by the smell of him.

With no sign of the creeper and more sober minds about, including three helmeted city sentries, Carolle asked, "You'll be all right here, Luce?"

Knocking on the blade up her sleeve, Lucille set her jaw and urged

Carolle on.

"All right," Carolle said. "Don't leave this spot." Pretending to retie the pink taffeta ribbons of her cuffs, Carolle paced closely to the warehouse's barn doors but heard little beyond what might have been sawing. She put her ear to the door.

"Oh, dear," someone moaned behind her.

Carolle gasped. "Rodinger!" She laid her hand over her heart. She hardly recognized him, dressed as plainly in wool as she, excluding his gray velvet gloves.

"I hope you were not waiting long. I realized I was cutting it fine as I departed."

"Not really. Where did you come from so sudden, like?"

He dabbed a kerchief to his forehead. "A secret for another time. After all, this is Trône d'Argent, my dear Carolle. A high lord cannot be seen dressed like the masses he's meant to represent." He winked to assure her it was in jest. "Shall we?" His cane rapped against the warehouse doors.

"Eh?" a voice screeched from inside.

"Breaking crests to mend ties," Rodinger said to the crack between the doors.

They slid apart a few inches, then parted enough to allow Rodinger entry. An armored guard bent and backed away, revealing the indoor shipyard. Carolle followed Rodinger inside and away from the other guards hidden behind the doors. Sawdust wafted through and speckled the air where sunlight broke through poorly covered windows. Scaffolding framed a sleek vessel-to-be on tracks extending into the bay at the end of the warehouse.

"Welcome, my lord," a wiry apprentice said. "Master Popplewell is—"

"Rodinger!" a blond pik called from high upon the scaffolding. "I'll be right down."

"Is this your ship?" Carolle asked.

"Yes and no," Rodinger answered. They moved to intercept the pik descending the scaffolding. "This remarkable vessel shall carry me and—more importantly—the treaties required for the Bonded Nations. Under the auspices of Queen Ameera and Queen Valentia of Virtud Luz, mages and boatbuilders alike rotate shifts to keep the construction on target for the spring."

In a work shirt and stained trousers, the clean-shaven pik landed with a grin. Stout with muscles, but short for his kind, he appeared even shorter next to Rodinger, standing only as tall as the middle of his thigh.

The pik extended his smudged hand up to Rodinger, who accepted without hesitation. "Master Popplewell has done us proud," Rodinger said. "But what else should we expect from the royal engineer?"

Master Popplewell threw back the compliment with both hands. "I'm learning as I go. As I keep rippin' reminding you, I'm no bloody shipwright, Rodinger."

"And as I keep repeating, Willem, it's my life on the waves out there. I prefer it to be your prototype whisking me about over the depths, if you do not mind."

The engineer swatted Rodinger's shin and raised a finger at him. "Don't you pin me with pride! That'll seal your doom for certain." Grinning again, he asked, "What brings you my way this morning?"

"Showing my dear friend around," Rodinger said. "I had hoped Lady Ysbryd and I could borrow your pier for some privacy." His gloved hand moved with his introduction.

Master Popplewell wrapped himself in his arms and beamed up at the incomplete behemoth. "Try not to judge my little miss too harshly without her armor on, Lady Ysbryd. She'll soon be the pride of our fleet, fastest ship on Cyr! We're building her to face the wind better than a carrack and warding her against ill waves and spells alike. Gods willing, she'll deliver our man here from port to port in a deft and boring fashion."

"I'd trust her over a coracle any day, Master Popplewell," Carolle replied.

"Confound it!" a whiny voice yelled from above. A Racinian mage placed his hands on his hips, puffing out his silver mantle. At his side, a Luzian in the Tower of Rosamond's crimson knelt near the incomplete hull. "Enunciate! Enunciate! It's a wonder your kind hold your borders at all."

The Luzian mage rose to puff out his mantle in turn. "You think I cast a spell to seal it? This is what you think? I should seal it before it has even been warded?" He flung his arm up in a rude dismissal.

"Ay! Gag it up there!" Master Popplewell yelled. "We've a lady in our company today." The royal engineer climbed. "You fizzlepots are worse than my children! I've already separated you once."

The mages placated the engineer with a waved apology before the Racinian peeled away.

Master Popplewell hung by one arm from the scaffolding. "If you have time when you're done, Rodinger, I'd like to share a few modifications we've made to the stern." Rodinger agreed and headed off toward the end of the warehouse. "Pleasure to meet you, Lady Ysbryd. Come back to see her when she's cutting waves. Legends will surround the Nymphony." He sat on a plank to shrug. "Or she may sink within minutes. Either way, you'll hear of her again."

Carolle smiled, waved to Master Popplewell, and sped to Rodinger's side. Longer than a galleon, the slender-framed ship would be quite the sight when completed. "The Nymphony?" Carolle asked, unable to keep her amusement from her lips. "Did you choose that name?"

"A lady at ease with the harmony of the seas?" Rodinger asked with a furrowed brow. "Is there something wrong with it?" Her mouth opened for an apology before he winked. "No, no. Willem names his creations. Won't take on a project without that caveat."

Stepping out of the lord's way, the bulky shipbuilders chanted their song along the tracks to the sea, a lowlander tune she'd heard but didn't know the name of. Not a one betrayed a snicker or a sneer for Rodinger.

"But the ship is yours?" she asked.

Rodinger raised a finger for her to hold the question. Approaching a series of ropes and pulleys, he selected one and let his weight do the tugging.

The strident hinges of a grand folding wall bent a panel forward to reveal the bay. Enamored of the salty breeze, Carolle swept down a wooden pier to the railing at its end, so weathered it had cracked and warped. Ships of every scale filled their white sails in the bright daylight under the mountains.

"To answer your question," Rodinger said, gathering his cloak about him, "the Nymphony is being created solely for the purpose of bringing the nations together. At the end of my voyage, I'm afraid she is meant as a gift in a stratagem poor Willem is not privy to. What shall happen to her afterward, I cannot say. Besides, I already own an oft-forgotten ship." He grunted and rolled his eyes. "Ooh, I say, I am odious, aren't I? Boasting like a fool when I brought you here under the pretenses of civility and candor."

"Actually, I'm sorry," Carolle said. "Embarrassed myself and my troupe at the gala, I did."

"Some may view it that way," Rodinger said. "But how many in attendance can purport Patevians are craven now?"

She laughed with little more than a hum and laid her hand on his shoulder. "Perhaps, but it's not the way a lady is supposed to behave, is it?"

"I disagree. You were forthright. In fact, I wish more Racinian women behaved as Patevian women do. I'm sure the queen could be persuaded to trade you for Lady Leupp, if you suggest it." His eyebrow arched jokingly, suggesting she consider it.

Carolle smirked but shook her head. "There's lovely. But I can't wish that on Patevia."

"I'm sorry for even mentioning her name." Gesturing back to the obscured ship, he said, "I, too, shall find myself battling specious nationality in unfamiliar courts. Without fellowship beyond my own confidence . . ." He leaned against the railing to exhale. "Confidence is a flighty thing, isn't it? Ameera praises my métier for smoothing ardent arguments into guileless conversation, yet I have my doubts." He splayed his hands. "I declined her request to take up this voyage three times."

"Can't imagine saying no to a queen, especially her."

"Ameera has been patient with me," he said. "Her father considered me a debauched thorn in his side." No one roamed within twenty yards of them, but he lowered his voice anyway. "There was a time when I didn't involve myself in politics, preferring to pursue sensualist, drunken endeavors. I think it was easier to live in that sickness. Thankfully, King Clyde's daughter gained a compassionate perspective during her time in the Tower and refuses to let us temporizing arseholes hide."

Footsteps on the pier urged Carolle to hold her questions. "My lord, my lady," Master Popplewell's young apprentice said, offering two saucers with steaming cups of tea. "Compliments of Master Popplewell."

Rodinger received his and tapped the porcelain cup to hers.

A biting wind gusted the steam away for her. She took a sip and cringed at the bitter strength. Rodinger made a face of disgust behind the apprentice's back. When the boy thudded back down the pier, Rodinger said, "I had thought you may appreciate this location more than chess and dinner. However, this tea may slay your enjoyment of the view."

"Never," Carolle replied, defiantly raising her cheek bones to the sea breeze. She set the saucer on the railing. "I've seen what Racine calls an afternoon tea. I can only guess what dinner involves. No. No, I suppose I can't imagine anything of that nature."

"Ah, yes, well. In my decades of experience, close friends make the best companions for High House dinners, inasmuch as the events are prone to cutting remarks and to tossing bread rolls in frustration—or once a full turkey—though amends must always be made over puddings and sherry."

"If you put it that way," Carolle said, "it sounds inviting. A cozy meal with the family, like."

"In many ways, it is, for those of us who have little family remaining." He twirled the black tea in his cup. "As a matter of fact, family is part of the reason this task with the Bonded Nations falls on my shoulders. My cousin Perry Boddlehock, the duke of Ghest in Critz, is one of the Warring States' most influential leaders. With the aid of the Nymphony, we hope he can persuade the less governmental states to join the fold."

"Why for did you agree to go?" Carolle asked. "What changed your mind?"

Baffled, Rodinger squeezed his bushy eyebrows together. "Why, you did, Carolle. Your performance."

She looked away to the bay.

"It inspired me. The heart you display as Elysant reminds me of something I lost twenty years back. A purity my daughter embodied. You may have gathered this, but you remind me a great deal of her."

Closing her eyes, Carolle released a sad moan. "I'm so sorry, Rodinger. I didn't know you had lost her."

"It was war," he said. "Lekelith demanded their independence after our king's tyrannical play for—well, never mind that. The lowlanders weren't selective when it came to targets; anything involving Racinian nobility worked, including a passenger galleon with a high lady and her daughter.

"The men responsible became my focus. One by one, my men and I found them and stretched their necks. When it was done . . ." His attention went back to swirling his drink. "My heart contains regrets aplenty, dear Carolle. I've been empty and angry for a very long time."

Rodinger didn't speak again until Carolle forced herself to look at him. "You remind me so much of Rose," he said. "Elegant and strong, with those cordial brown eyes."

Carolle shifted her stance against the rail, feeling the awkward flush of the compliment. "If you hired a harlot in Deganwy, I may actually be your daughter."

The High House noble stood erect, drawing his arm back.

Carolle's cheeks blazed. "I'm sorry. I don't know why I said that, really."

Nodding politely, Rodinger resumed his lean against the railing, which creaked in protest. "I suspect I do. Sadly, I cannot claim to be your father, though I would find great pride in it." He nudged her with his elbow. She refused to look at him, merely ran a grin over her lips. "Knowing your origin and where you stand today, can you not believe yourself worthy of the compliment? Your strength cannot be unknown to you when it's so evident to the rest of us."

Carolle watched the waves lap against the posts beneath them. Strength enough not to betray him? Gods, the man had become a friend, and truly believed her a confidante. And the coin . . .

Rodinger's tea splashed into the frothing sea. "My apologies to the fishes," he said.

She tipped her cup over with a small smile. "I should get back to the theatre for practice." Her eyes met his adoration but swiftly swept over the bay again. "Thank you for sharing this with me." She dipped.

"I've made you uncomfortable."

Raising her hand, she cut off his apology. "I am better for it. Ta." She turned to go.

Rodinger said, "Elysant on the Glass owes its origins to a people long gone and gods who ignore our pleas today. Yet we understand, wordlessly, the emotions fueling the passion you embody in your dance. That sympathy—empathy, really—is the thread to bind us all. I had forgotten it, believed it beyond my reach." He took her hand in his soft gloves and brought her around to face him. "Spreading that understanding is my calling now. If I am successful, the world should thank you."

"Stop," Carolle replied. "They should thank your Rose. Her memory inspired you, Rodinger."

His brow creased. "Dinner?" he asked. "We can hide from our reputations and rubrics in my house and discuss this when the rolls are nice and hard."

Squeezing his velvet-gloved hand, she said, "I look forward to your invitation."

"Invitation?" he repeated. He didn't follow her into the sawdust-covered warehouse, or at least didn't catch up to her. She heard Master Popplewell summon him but refused to look back.

Carolle Ysbryd belonged on stage. Each time she stepped off, she found trouble with these world-molders, pulling her into realms where she didn't belong.

The barn doors drew open. Carolle's heart chugged when Grand Diviner Sylvester came inside. Dressed as a labor-stained farmer with a smear of muck on his cheek for good measure, the man had disguised himself well enough but missed the mark with his barn owl. Omelet's pink muffin cap didn't make toting around an owl less conspicuous. Carolle sidled by him, feeling the mage's intense curiosity on her.

In the crowded street, she forced a smile as Lucille unknowingly hurried toward a fight. There was no getting past it now. She didn't want to know the truth of Gaines's motives for going after Rodinger and the Warring States.

Yes, it couldn't be helped. She would send word to Gaines and return his father's plat. Curse nobles! And curse their bloody, bloody coin!

Chapter 8: Golden Threats

Carolle peeled off her glowing costume, dropped it in front of the mirror, and fell into the only chair in their bedchamber. She propped her sore feet on her bed. Braith brought over a tray with heated oil and soap.

Lucille wrung out a steaming rag and laid it over the mouth of the ewer on the bath stand. "I'm only saying you should hear Gaines out." Carolle's glower didn't deter her. "Don't do something rash, like. I'm not being funny; that plat can do a proper lot of good. In your hands."

"In my hands? You're doing my head in, Luce. I couldn't do what Rodinger can." Carolle poured the olive oil over the pitch on her chest and began to rub it in. "Gaines and his father'll use whatever I tell them against our own queen's wishes—against the Bonded Nations. I'm sure of it."

"The Bonded Nations?" Lucille asked, passing over the damp rag. "Who's getting ahead of herself now? We're talking about one noble and the Warring States. You can't know what'll occur—"

"I can! Because I won't do it!" Carolle wiped the last of the olive oil from her chest and slung the rag to the tray. "I'm not my mam! I'm not a whore!"

Lucille's cheeks went ruddy. "I was. The women who reared you were! You look down on them now, do you?"

"Course not, Luce bach." Carolle sat forward. "I'm only saying Gaines is buying a part of me that's not for sale, man. No coin should give me pause over that."

Braith said to her fidgeting fingers, "Really makes you a mercenary more than a prostitute, doesn't it?"

Carolle defied Lucille's glare with her own and responded with an audible sigh through her nose.

Someone gently tapped twice at the door. It cracked open. "Braith, love?" Dafydd asked. Braith scurried to block his view.

Lucille draped her cloak over Carolle. They sat opposite each other with softened features. "There'll be Gaines," Lucille whispered.

"I never wanted to feel this way," Carolle said. "The way that coin makes me feel."

Lucille sulked and studied her hands in her lap.

"This is what's best, Luce."

Braith put her back to the door and offered a reassuring smile. "It's not Gaines. Madame Davies wants a word, Carolle. I told Dafydd you'll be there now in a minute."

Dressed as herself, Carolle sought out Madame Davies in the suites upstairs and found her sitting at her vanity. A letter preoccupied her thoughts among the plentiful bouquets. "Madame Davies?"

"Never thought you the type, Carolle bach," she said without looking up. "To marry into security." Carolle took the note. Rodinger's formal invitation to dinner.

Madame Davies waved away her words. "I'm not saying I disagree with your methods. I shouldn't be surprised. You've always taken care of yourself more than the rest have done."

"If that were true, I wouldn't be in the troupe." Carolle laid the note aside and stood behind her matron. She began removing hairpins from the older woman's lavender-perfumed curls. "Lord Bernard is a friend, not a suitor."

Madame Davies's cackle dwindled into a chortle. "Oh, you should see your cheeks, good girl! Beet red! You can't fool me. And before you go denying it again, recall I saw you spending your time with High Lord Bernard in the castle the night of the gala. The way he jumped to your defense, like."

"I don't remember that," Carolle said into the mirror. "After all you've done for me, Madame Davies, and Queen Ada, I can't imagine why I'd want to marry out of this life."

"You do it for security, of course! Servants dipping and bowing, bringing you grapes and wine and feather pillows . . ." She snapped herself out of her daydream. "Got to be honest with you, Carolle Ysbryd, you could belong in that world. Your heart knows it. You didn't want to be a dancer, either. But fate has served you well."

"That's different. I chose to be the Pixie of Bryn Mawr. I liked being a footpad. And I thought I'd be sent to the gallows if I didn't agree."

Madame Davies softened her expression. "That's as may be, yet someone's lit a fire inside you, girl. Can you honestly say you'd go back to that life if you left this one? No, you can't. Sometimes fate puts you where you need to be. Gods know I didn't plan on spending my middle years minding troublins day in, day out."

Carolle's embarrassment roasted. She set the last pin on the vanity. "I belong with you lot. I'm a hard worker. What work is there in being carted around to mingle with the like who can't disagree without waving a fan?"

Madame Davies didn't seem to hear her, contemplating behind her faint grimace. "Older than I would've expected, mind. But a high lord of the Tenth Ring has ways to compensate for that."

"Please, Madame Davies. I remind him of his late daughter." Carolle knelt next to her matron. "I want to stay with you and someday start my own troupe. Your life is far more appealing than peeled grapes."

"Ha!" Madame Davies said to her reflection. "You hear this? She's sending us to an early grave. Taking our lives for our livelihood." She began scrubbing away at her makeup.

Carolle rose to meet her gaze in the mirror. "Never. I want to do what you do. Help those in need, in trouble."

Madame Davies patted Carolle's hand and shrugged. "We'll see, won't we?" She resumed her scrubbing. Carolle took up the invitation and departed the floral scents of the room.

Out in the hallway, Dafydd waited for her. "Braith sent me. There's a Lord Gaines in the theatre to see you." He followed her. "If I'm going to be running up and down by here delivering your messages, I may start expecting some coin—"

Her sharp look cut him off. He couldn't have meant the plat. Braith wouldn't have told him. "Sorry, Dafydd. I'm having a demanding evening, as you know."

Traipsing the hall's creaky floorboards with her, he said, "This Gaines feller looks like a right twat. You want me to go with you?"

"I'll be fine, ta." Then she reflected on what refusing a noble may bring. "But if I'm not back in a few, I wouldn't mind if you checked in on me."

He agreed with a furrowed brow. She didn't have the time to explain.

Back in her quarters, Lucille and Braith grew silent when she entered. Lucille had Gaines's purse in her hands. She held it out to Carolle. "One hundred and fifty little coins. All counted and ready to go." Her grip wasn't easily conquered.

Carolle said, "It is for the best, biwt. Wish me luck?"

Gazing longingly at the purse, Lucille gave a weak agreement. "Aye. Go on. You've already kept him waiting."

"Good luck!" Braith shouted as Carolle thudded down the hallway with the hefty purse in her arms.

From backstage, Carolle spied into the theatre and saw no one. A crack brought her attention to the royal box. There Gaines sat, tossing nutshells on the floor.

Carolle doubled back and hesitated for a moment outside the royal crests on the curtains. She entered. Gaines rose and examined her woolen gown as she did the same for the bruise—or bruises—overtaking the left side of his face. When his eyes lit on the purse, he deflated back to his chair.

"What happened to you?" Carolle asked. "Is that why for you missed the gala?"

Side-eyeing the purse, Gaines said, "I live a charmed life. More charmed by the minute, it seems." He jammed his hand into a sack of nuts in the chair next to him. A purse identical to the one Carolle carried lay on the chair as well.

She set her purse with its twin and sat in the next chair over. "Oh, don't be embarrassed, man. Worse things have happened at sea. I hope he— or she—got theirs."

Gaines exhaled loudly. "He. He always gets his and never accepts less than what he wants. Especially in rebuke." Abruptly sitting forward, he scanned the theatre and listened for a moment. Relaxing, he popped a hazelnut in his mouth and gave it a meaningful chomp.

With the tip of his belt knife, he bored into the soft part of another shell and said, "I've been informed you learnt something interesting about Lord Bernard's association with the Warring States."

"What? By who?" Carolle asked. "The man in the gray mask?"

Gaines put his finger to his mouth to shush her. He leaned over the purses to whisper. "No! We don't speak of them. If you ever see one, you run the other way." She felt a bit dizzy from the fear in his voice, but nodded. He sat back and raised his eyebrows, prompting her to tell him what she had learned.

She gathered the wool of her skirt in her fists. "I don't know how interesting it is to hear he's cousins with a duke. Figured you'd already know that."

He studied her reaction and pouted his disappointment. "There's more to it than that, isn't there?"

"Well that's as may be," she said. "I can't help you. If I'm honest, noble acts are more appealing than noble coin. I'm sorry. Here's your purse. I kindly ask you to leave me be." Carolle rose.

Gaines brushed the splintered hazelnut shells from his lap to clatter to the floor. "No, I don't think so. I'm sorry too. I cannot let you go yet, Carolle Graean."

Splinters of frost drove through Carolle's chest upon hearing her name. Her mouth went dry. Crossing her arms to counter his apology, she said, "I wouldn't have believed you to be the brave sort, Barimor Gaines. But here you are, alone, speaking things you shouldn't be."

That brought the haughtiness back to his tanned, yellow-and-purple-bruised face. "Brave enough to be alone with a penniless footpad? The bastard daughter of a brothel whore?" He stood as she tried on Queen Ameera's steely expression. "Does the elegant Carolle Ysbryd not want to be reminded of her harlot mother? Good. I'd want to distance myself from the fate of joining those diseased harpies, too." He kicked the chair holding the purses.

"What will it take to get rid of you?" Carolle asked.

His features apologized again, tempting her to darken his other eye. "Keep your word," he said, stowing his knife. Gaines dug into his jerkin pocket for his snuff case and tapped a deposit onto the back of his hand. "Don't desert me like some elf. Tell me what you know." Carolle took a step up while he snorted the brown powder. "Don't desert your Madame Davies, either. Rumors place thieves and prostitutes in your troupe—"

"What are you saying?"

Gaines twitched his nose and closed his case. "Queen Ada has a strange sense of humor, sending your kind across borders," he said and returned the snuff to his pocket. "The problem your matron faces is that simply bringing a troupe of miscreants into Racine carries a precedent, one that puts you and your troupe in pillories and sends your 'madame' to the gallows. Did I hear correctly that Queen Ameera announced Racine's entry into the Bonded Nations with the woman standing behind her?" He scrubbed a hand under his nose. "To illustrate my point, that murderer in your midst, Lord Dafydd Gallivan—"

"Shut up! You don't know what you're saying. Braith's father abused her. Come after them, and I'll lump you myself! Wretch!"

"Save him," Gaines growled back. "You could save all of these dancers who are one misstep away from a brothel." He came closer, letting the light reveal his busted lip. "Carolle?"

"You keep my name out of your mouth." Her heated stare weighed him. He genuinely seemed to be struggling with his threats. "Who did that to you? Who's making you do this?"

"Someone who can make us both disappear if I fail."

Carolle's frustration summoned tears she blinked back.

Gaines murmured, "We have no choice."

"I understand that!" Carolle snapped. Her fingers rubbed the invitation in her hand. She fanned herself with it. Upon realizing what she was doing, she quit and groaned. How long has she been here for that to become a habit? Too long. Too long around cockin' nobles. "In Popplewell's warehouse, they're building a ship. The Nymphony. Warding it with magic, like. It's a gift for Lord Bernard's cousin, the duke of Ghest in Critz."

Understanding dawned in Gaines's eyes. "Smart. Intimidate Crestwall into joining. Miltiad legally cannot refuse. The other Warring States won't resist Crestwall, Miltiad, and Critz."

Gaines passed her on the steps. "You've nearly earned your coin and your freedom, Lady Ysbryd."

"Nearly?"

"One last task." He faced her from the curtained entrance. "The final. You have my word. My request is this: accept Lord Bernard's invitation."

Carolle pinched the invitation tighter. "Why for?"

"To save him," Gaines answered, "just like you're saving your troupe. Do what you can—all that you can—and keep him in his High House tomorrow, far away from the docks. The death of a high lord is more attention than they'll want, but they'll achieve their goal no matter the price."

Her stomach gurgled, promising illness. "Gaines, could we stand against them?"

A hopeful hesitation lingered, but he closed his eyes and shook his head. "Save your troupe, Lady Ysbryd, and keep Lord Bernard from interfering with the destruction of his ship."

Her thoughts erupted. "They work day and night. Guarded. They'll always be there. Then they'll just build another—" Unless they couldn't. "You won't hurt Master Popplewell! Give me your word!"

"You think I have a say?" he growled. He stood there for a moment. "Console yourself with your new coin or imagine your troupe dancing in fetters. Lady's choice. Either way, don't waver now. You're almost free." He ripped the crested curtains down, wadded them into a ball, and threw them aside.

Carolle waited until Gaines was gone and bade Dafydd a good night at the entrance to the back of the house. Then she collected the purses and brought them to the costumery. Alone with her thoughts, Carolle circled until her mind fell silent and her core numb. Whatever Gaines intended for the Nymphony, steal the designs or burn it, she wouldn't betray her troupe for a ship. Master Popplewell . . . they'd have to start anew, on a new ship. But Rodinger would be safe at home.

After combining the coins into one purse, Carolle hid it beneath a scenery cart. Her shaking hand penned the acceptance to Rodinger's invitation. With that carried off, she returned to her dark quarters and sat on her bunk. Carolle leaned forward and opened the empty purse for Lucille and Braith. "Done," she whispered. "We don't bother with Gaines now."

Lucille moped but got up to give Carolle a hug.

"This doesn't change anything, Luce," Braith said, lying on her side.

"We can still carry on like before."

"I know," Lucille said weakly. "I do hope Chester has more sense than his friend do."

Perhaps Chester was part of the "they" Gaines feared. That didn't seem right. Chester had been subservient to Gaines when they'd met them.

"What?" Lucille asked.

Realizing she stared, Carolle answered, "Nothing. I'm just worried for you. You'll have to deal with that lot while you're being courted. Gods, for the rest of your life, if you marry the man."

"Bite your tongue," Braith whispered.

Lucille feigned offense. "You think I'd stick around when he's no longer fun?" They giggled. "I'll be right here with you. We can both be Madame Davies. I'm the talent and you're the loud crone."

Carolle elbowed Lucille off her bed and bade them a good night. Her mind worked the puzzle of Gaines's scheme and what it would truly mean for her troupe if she declined. To calm her nerves, she wound and rewound the thin chain of the dragon's ear through her fingers.

When Lucille's snoring steadied, Carolle slid off her blankets, snatched up her boots, and made her way back to the purse hidden in the costumery. One thing she could see clearly, it wasn't safe anywhere in the theatre. Gaines or his cohorts might report she had stolen it now that they knew of her past.

In need of concealment and agility, Carolle donned a pair of dark blue trousers and a matching tunic. She sneaked past Mage Serrano's private room, where he and Madame Davies were celebrating with their second bottle of wine, judging by the murmured words and tender cooing. She pressed on to the alley.

In a wintry drizzle, the freedom of the night hit her as solidly as the wind up the bay. Clutching the purse to her side, she rounded Theatre Row to Port Way and stuck to the shadows as best she could, hiding behind crates, carts, and barrels whenever someone wandered by on her way to the Temple District. No one out at the peak of night could be up to good doings.

Carolle thanked the gods when she finally found the squat temple to Pencer, the pik god of the feasts. Around back, she tiptoed to the pair of short black doors, the Portals to Shadow. Humans believed the little people had added them as a false entrance, a memorial to Pencer's slain twin sister, Panette, the goddess of shadows. But Carolle had relied on the truth of the Portals more than once. For if there was a race worth their word, it was the piks.

Certain she wasn't seen, Carolle crouched inside. A tiny corridor sloped downhill to a small brazier and two pik guards. At the sight of a human, the guards peeled their pale eyes and seized the hilts of their daggers.

Time to see if Liliwen had spoken truthfully when she'd said the Patevian password would be accepted around the world. "A ddwg ŵy a ddwg fwy," she said to the older guard. His hand lifted from his dagger to scratch his scalp through his leather cap.

"What?" the younger guard asked. Pointing the sprig of whiskers on his chin at Carolle, he drew his blades fully.

The older pik translated, "He who steals an egg will steal more." He thwacked his companion on the back of his helmet. "She's Patevian, Rumer. You need to study up, lad." The older guard waved Carolle forward. "Segurdod yw clod y cledd." A sword's credit is its idleness.

"I'll be needing your vault, gentlemen," Carolle said.

Pursing his lips, Rumer shifted his weight forward to stand on the balls of his feet. "No sudden moves, human. The slowest of our kind is always quicker than the fastest of yours."

"Not when it comes to wit," said his partner. He put his fingers to the stone wall.

Rumer frowned over at him and palmed a stone himself. They pressed and rotated the stones in unison. A hidden door swung open behind Rumer, revealing a smaller opening than the cramped corridor in which Carolle hunched. Rumer led the way as Carolle crawled on all fours down the steep decline into the stale air. The door behind her resealed before the floor leveled out.

"How does a human know our secrets?" Rumer asked.

At the end of the tunnel, the ceiling allowed Carolle to stand again. She brushed the dust and grit from her hands and said, "A friend told me."

The wheels in Rumer's head spun. "Then they're a tossin' traitor! This isn't a secret to share. Never with humans!"

"When I was twelve, I saved her daughter from drowning in the river, man. She didn't have coin but wanted to repay me." That cooled his steam a bit.

They walked past three tiers of pik-high openings on either side of the corridor. Ladders on rails offered access to those higher in the walls. Carolle sought one that didn't have a small stone at the entrance, marking it as claimed.

Spotting a stone-free hole, Carolle rolled a ladder near. Again, she'd have to crawl. She threw the purse into the ancient vault first and awkwardly managed to shuffle inside from halfway up the ladder.

Rumer hoisted a lantern on a pole in order for her to see. Thankfully, the vault went only as deep as her height. After depositing the purse on one of the embedded shelves, she removed the dragon's ear from around her neck and set the necklace on a shelf of its own.

Scooting back out on her backside, she dropped down to where Rumer was setting the lantern on its pedestal. He selected a stone from a pile beneath the light and offered her the tan river rock. "I was wrong. She was right to tell an ally to our people."

The statement gave Carolle pause, conjuring thoughts of her betrayal of Master Popplewell. Setting the rock at the edge of the vault, Carolle said, "I didn't save her son." They didn't speak again.

Along the bay, Carolle roamed in the mist. Carolle Graean or Carolle Ysbryd? Master Popplewell's cheery face interrupted her thoughts. Poor dab. May the gods—the world—forgive her.

Chapter 9: An Evening in Crimson

No smoke rose from the west end of the docks into the ribbons of coral sky. Supporting herself with the balcony's balustrade, Carolle exhaled a relieved breath and fogged the sunset. Master Popplewell's face appeared in her mind's eye again. Her yellow long-sleeved gown served no protection against that chill.

"Carolle?" Rodinger asked, waiting for an answer to a question she hadn't heard. "I asked if you'd care for a game while we wait for our meal."

If she acted now, said something, perhaps she could save Master Popplewell. And doom her troupe. The weight of her thoughts must have reached her face; Rodinger frowned in concern.

"A pleasure to defeat you again," she said, "if that's what you're after."

"A bold claim!" he said.

Carolle kept an eye on the port as they made their way inside. From the upstairs gallery, Rodinger guided her into the odor of pipe smoke lingering in his study. A stout desk in the same dark oak as the wainscoting filled the back of the room. Beyond stood a grand fireplace and shelves laden with curiosities. Snagged instantly, Carolle perused the wonders, running her fingers over the treasures: geodes in sea green, ivory tusks, and ancient weapons far too brittle for battle now.

When she touched a blowpipe engraved with frogs, Rodinger said, "That is a gift from High Lord Swinton's travels. Many of these baubles come from the first largess he received in his exploration of the desert regions." He went to a mahogany chess table and arranged its stone figures.

Behind the table, a gold-framed, life-sized portrait of two women hung on the wall. The plaque lured Carolle closer to read LADY MADELINE AND LADY ROSE OF HIGH HOUSE BERNARD, TENTH RING. Both ladies shared her brown eyes. With Lady Rose's broad lips, she and Carolle could have believably passed as sisters.

Dressed in the pastel fashion of the year, Lady Madeline's hair had gone white, and Lady Rose appeared older than the queen. Rodinger couldn't be old enough for them to have died looking like this twenty years ago. "Is this new?" Carolle asked.

Rodinger's cheeks colored. "I paint them each season, as I imagine they would appear today."

Her face warmed in sympathy. Leaning in closer, Carolle studied his daughter. "Talented, you are," she said encouragingly. "If your daughter's name is Rose, why for is she holding a frost lily?"

"Our favorite," Rodinger said, holding his finger back from caressing the blue flower with frosted white petals. "They bloom from around her birthday on through Winter Peak."

"Well," Carolle said, curtsying to the painting. "Lady Madeline and Lady Rose, I welcome your support in my game against Lord Bernard."

Bolstered, Rodinger barked, "Ha! You may have the support of my rival, the Lady Rose, but no one shall turn my wife against me." He pulled Carolle's chair out from beneath the chessboard.

Moving through a few memorized plays, Carolle discovered that forcing a distraction from her worries wasn't helpful. Thoughts of Master Popplewell arose whenever Rodinger deliberated on his next move. "Sad, innit?" Carolle asked. "Mathanas has to fall for me to conquer Triumph."

Rodinger clacked down a wave to distract her from Pliman. Then he heard what she said. His head tilted as an amused smirk appeared. "Are you still imagining characters from your show as the game pieces? Is that why you are so protective of this pawn? A 'canary,' yes? And that bard I'll be taking in a turn or two?"

"I'll thank you kindly to be leaving my friends alone, good boy."

Thackeray, Rodinger's wrinkled servant, apparently the only personal attendant Rodinger had kept on permanently in recent years, marched into the room. "Your dinner is ready, Lord Bernard."

"We'll be with you in one moment, Thackeray," Rodinger replied. To Carolle, he asked, "Shall we end this?" His eyes crinkled with a restrained laugh at her perplexed study of the board. "Remember, you do not have to collect all of the pieces to win." Rodinger's forefinger scooted Elysant back three squares, diagonally trapping Triumph between her and his siblings. "Ah, dear me. Bother. Arse. Checkmate for you, it seems."

Thackeray had vacated the gallery by the time they emerged from Rodinger's study. As they crossed into the long dining room, Carolle wondered how many of the happy portraits in the gallery Rodinger had painted.

A feast of salmon, crabs, goose, and small plates awaited them between the blackened embroidery of twenty-four straight-backed chairs. Carolle inspected the gallery behind her. "Are we expecting an army?"

"Regrettably detained, it would seem."

Surveying the table's offerings, Carolle teased, "Why, High Lord Rodinger Bernard, I do believe you are afraid of me."

"What makes you say that?"

"There's not a single roll on this table, man," Carolle answered. "What am I supposed to toss in the throes of my impassioned tantrum? Is that what the goose is for?"

Night brightened the candlelight while they dined. Conversation served to distract Carolle from her betrayal for a few minutes here and there. But as the meal progressed, it resurfaced, each time with more potency, making it harder to ignore the looming treachery. When Rodinger wasn't looking, she lifted her hair off her neck and fanned herself with her hand. Her hair had dampened with sweat. She rose from the table.

"Are you all right?" Rodinger asked, standing.

All but running out of the room, she replied, "Oh, aye. Ate too much. Just need a little fresh air." She forced herself to wait for Rodinger's escort to the balcony.

The cool air soothed her stomach as she walked directly to the balustrade facing the west end of the bay. Below the moonlit mountains, harbor lamps roughly outlined the dark patch where Popplewell's warehouse stood. No fires yet; they would surely burn a ship if they meant to destroy it.

"Coffee, my lord?" Thackeray asked from behind them.

"Splendid idea, Thackeray," Rodinger answered. He explained to Carolle, "A delightful remedy for languid spirits." While Rodinger went on about the origin of the coffee, another of Lord Swinton's finds, Carolle drank in the cold. Perhaps Gaines had chosen to stand up for decency? For peace. She hadn't. Her fist pounded the balustrade.

Thackeray set cups and a pot covered in silver acanthus leaves on a small folding table and retreated to the archway. Rodinger poured the steaming dark liquid. As he held out her cup, his face slackened. He dropped it. It shattered. "What in the world . . .?"

Orange light flickered in the bay. Flames danced high. They doubled. Carolle's heart sank as the blaze spread through the docks. Bells pealed.

The alarm swelled, ringing up Verdict Hill. Rodinger said, "I'm afraid our evening must come to an end, Carolle. I'm needed on the docks."

"No, Rodinger, don't," Carolle said to his surprise. "You'll make yourself a target for the vandals."

He waved Thackeray over and sent him away to bring back Carolle's cloak and fan. "I must know what damage has been done and report to the queen. That jolly well could be Popplewell's warehouse. Best to get you back to the theatre before this commotion wakes the whole city."

She dug her fingers into his cambric sleeve to stall him. Shouts joined the ringing from down the hill. Rodinger gripped her arm tightly and said, "Do not fear for me. I shall bring the guard."

"Then take me with you," she replied, unable to conjure an excuse to hold him longer. Reluctantly, he agreed, though she could tell he worked on an argument to talk her out of it. Good, she could still slow him down.

He returned her hand to the balustrade. "Where is Thackeray?"

Carolle let him go on alone, scheming on how to keep him in his High House. Her thoughts jumped to hope for Master Popplewell's rescue. An unwelcome notion reminded her the engineer made a better target than his construct.

A sinewy blue line coiled out of the bay's depths. Trône d'Argent's mighty water dragon crested his green fins down his back. A great breath from Harishnu's bearded maw propelled a cloud of mist and jets of water onto the hungry flames. Within seconds, the light extinguished. Cheers rose to challenge the bells until the ringing ceased altogether.

Carolle loosed her own wild cry in celebration. "Rodinger!" she shouted. "Harishnu doused the fire! Come see!" Blithe hope consumed her. There was a chance! Hope for Master Popplewell.

She ran into the High House. Upstairs, she cut off her call to Rodinger and froze. Behind a pink settee, an arm lay outstretched from beneath her cloak. Crumpling the silk brocade, Carolle threw it aside. Thackeray. He breathed but his arm had been badly broken. Blood stained his sleeve around the fracture. In stockinged feet, Carolle checked the dining room, then crossed the gallery to the study.

The chess table had been scooted away from the portrait of Rodinger's family. Between the golden frame and the wall was a sliver of darkness. Goose-pimpled and cold with fear, Carolle crept toward Lady Rose's gleeful portrayal and eased the frame outward, revealing a portal to dank blackness. A tunnel? "Rodinger?" she whispered into the dark. Carolle stood away from the portrait as she listened. No one answered.

Picking up a large tome from the desk, Carolle considered fleeing but dismissed the notion. She inched into the gallery, hunting for the slightest hint of Rodinger. A muffled cry set her feet running downstairs, leaping down steps past the balcony and into the residence of the High House.

At the entrance to Rodinger's bedchamber, she froze. Five hooded men in gray cloaks circled Rodinger before his lit fireplace. Rodinger clutched his knee on the plush rug and tried to stand with the aid of a chair. Gold leaf shone on the round heads of the maces blocking Rodinger's escape.

One of the men kicked over the chair, sending Rodinger to all fours. His attackers wore large-nosed gray porcelain masks, identical to the one she had seen in the alley across from Popplewell's. Her body tingled, urging her to do something. No matter Gaines's warning, she refused to flee. She wouldn't desert her friend.

Rodinger spotted her and moaned. "Run!"

"Run?" one of the men asked. "Lady Ysbryd kept you exactly where we needed you." Rodinger studied her. His denial faded quickly to hurt accusation as she tried to deny it beyond shaking her head. Without warning, the masked man swung his weapon.

"No!" Carolle screamed.

The men broke their circle and backed away from Rodinger's prone body. Carolle ran to him and dropped to her knees. Red drained from his brow. His exhale coated her arm in a warmth that faded with the wisdom in his blue eyes. He was gone, forever believing she'd betrayed him wittingly.

The cloaks skirted the walls, slinking toward the hallway. Carolle shielded herself with the tome and rose. "Mask yourself all you like; I know your form, Barimor Gaines!" The taller man next to him flinched. "Chester Fellows." The other gray masks swung to look at them. Slowly, silently, the three strangers backed away while pointing at Carolle. They entered the hallway and blocked the exit.

Carolle slung the tome at Gaines, cracking his mask over his bruise.

He snarled and tore off the broken porcelain. "You stupid woman! We waited until he was alone, for your sake!"

"What do we do, Gaines?" Chester whined as he circled Carolle. "She said our names."

"I know! Shut up!" Gaines shifted his weight and acknowledged the men outside the doorway with a slow nod. "No loose ends."

Carolle pounced for Gaines, but Chester struck first. She hit the parquet floor hard. Her ribs felt sharp. Wind stirred her hair. Darkness reigned.

Chapter 10: The Price of Salvation

Carolle groaned. Pain splintered deeper behind her temples. Her mouth tasted awful. Someone held her right arm. Her eyes opened and blinked to focus. Grand Diviner Sylvester sat next to her in the glaring morning light. Without his owl. On Rodinger's poster bed. She tried to pull away from him, but the ache in her side held her fast.

"You have poor timing," the grand diviner said. "You're going to wish you had slept through this treatment, too."

Gbad'Wu appeared on Carolle's left, her face concerned. "Wait!"

Grand Diviner Sylvester dropped a slimy stone covered in musky ground-herb filth onto her exposed belly. "Lukhuni ngamatye," he said. The stone burst. Carolle's bones grew heavy. Her skull, too hefty to hold up, sank into her pillow. She couldn't inhale! Grand Diviner Sylvester harbored no sympathy in his predatory watch. "Breathe later. Relax and let it work."

Black flecks speckled Carolle's vision. The spell released. Carolle gasped. Gbad'Wu picked up Carolle's left hand in both of hers and skewered the grand diviner with a glare.

"She's breathing," he said.

"Am I to applaud?" Gbad'Wu asked. "Does this end your experiment?"

Elanis watched with an intent frown from the foot of the bed. "It's been days, Gbad'Wu," she said. "It requires a few weeks at least. We agreed to this."

"The decision no longer rests with us, Elanis," the monk replied. Gbad'Wu climbed onto the edge of the down mattresses and rubbed Carolle's hand with her calloused fingers. "Carolle, how do you feel?"

"Lighter," Carolle managed. Her headache had eased a bit, letting her focus her vision and her mind. She searched the bedchamber. Only the fire moved. "Where to is Rodinger?"

"Mourn when the luxury of time is yours," Grand Diviner Sylvester said. "Who attacked you?"

"Mourn?" Carolle repeated, recalling Rodinger's fate.

"He's right," Elanis said distantly, almost coldly, as though the woman couldn't feel her own emotions. "Rodinger can rest easier in the Glades knowing those who tried to sabotage his cause have been brought to justice. Honor him by helping us find his assassins."

Carolle's head swam, though she clearly saw the accusation of betrayal in Rodinger's eyes. That's what coin brought her, as much happiness as it had ever brought her mam. Bloody, cockin' nobles! Gaines had said to keep Rodinger safe! Here! She blinked back her tears and let her anger flare for Gaines. "Well, where to is Madame Davies? She'll want to know I'm awake."

The grand diviner answered, "She's certainly not here. She believes you're dead."

"Have you no heart?" Gbad'Wu snapped at the old mage. She stroked Carolle's forearm and explained. "For your sake, the assassins must believe themselves successful. Queen Ameera announced your passing with Lord Bernard's."

Carolle rose to her elbows until her head retaliated with waves of pain. Between stabbing breaths, she asked, "So . . . I'm dead? My troupe thinks I'm dead?"

"Oui," the monk answered. "There were no alternatives, Carolle. You must understand." She tried to console Carolle with a smile.

"The monk is right," the grand diviner said. "The Filii Cinere do not leave witnesses." At the snap of his fingers, his owl swooped into the room and perched on his shoulder.

Carolle repeated, "Fee-lee chin-air . . .?"

"Filii Cinere," Gbad'Wu said. "Zealots who seek to restore Merith's rule over the continent, or something similar. Enslave magic. Enslave the poor. They ignite the bigotry within the people to divide them."

"Hence the masks of ancient King Vendral," Elanis added. "The very concept of the Bonded Nations opposes their creed; their interference was expected."

"Oui. Mais, not like this."

Elanis went to the fireplace and added some logs.

"If you kill them," Carolle thought aloud, "can I go back? Can I dance?"

The answer to Carolle's question came cordially from Gbad'Wu's face before Sylvester said, "You are better served remaining dead. Their numbers are secret, but your name is known to them. You'd get everyone close to you killed." Omelet focused on Gbad'Wu's piercing glare. "The reach of our enemy has been demonstrated, monk."

To the flames, Elanis said, "It is harsh not to give Rodinger—not to have time to mend your sorrows. To see your own death while you live . . . However, the perpetrators count on us licking our wounds. Three days have already passed since they attacked you."

Nodding her hesitant agreement, Gbad'Wu said, "Oui. Thackeray did not see his attackers. Did you?"

"Three days?" Carolle asked. "Thackeray is alive?"

"Yes, girl," the grand diviner said impatiently. "Now answer the question."

She crushed the cotton quilt with her free hand as she thought. Carolle Ysbryd was dead. Carolle Graean was dead. They knew both of her names. Rodinger was dead. She saw the hurt in his expression just before he died. Her intention had never been to betray him. Now she could only watch her own life from afar. Fury burned through her, charring her, swift and even and stoked by her pain. "There were three," she answered. Chester and Gaines would die by her hand! "They wore masks and cloaks. I didn't see their faces."

The grand diviner arched his thin eyebrow and groaned irritably.

Returning to the bed, Elanis tugged the hem of her silver mantle beneath her chest. Her gaze burrowed through her spectacles. "You saw nothing? A limp? A boot? The particular color of an iris? Try to remember any detail. Give us something to go on. What clothes did they wear beneath their cloaks?"

The owl turned to Carolle, waiting for an answer. "I don't know. I'm sorry."

"Liar," Sylvester said.

Carolle's whole face flushed. "What?"

"You saw it. Whether you remember it is a different matter."

"Then I don't remember."

"Better," he replied. "But also a lie." His bony right hand went up his left sleeve as far as his armpit and came back out with a steel butterfly on a ring. A faint golden glow filled the wings until he removed the end of his finger.

"What is this?" Gbad'Wu asked.

Elanis moved around the bed to his side for a better view. "Is that a butterfly of the Oculi?"

Gbad'Wu inclined her head slightly for an explanation.

"The god of insight—or the goddess of spies, depending on their mood."

Sylvester sighed. "Yes. Never trust a butterfly with a secret. But this shall help her remember." Sylvester reached for Carolle's hand. She pulled it back. "Don't be a coward."

That got Carolle up on her elbows. "Don't you call me that!"

The old mage smirked and pressed her shoulder back down. "Settle down. It's not invasive. The ring takes you back to that moment, so you can observe what you saw without your memory clouding your vision. Believe me; if I could go in there myself, I would."

Gbad'Wu stalled his second attempt and said in a tone with no room to argue, "She needs rest."

"No," Carolle said, extending her hand toward the small butterfly. "It's all right." If the others couldn't see the attack, her secret was safe, her vengeance guarded. "I want to bring Rodinger justice." And identify the three masked strangers.

Sylvester's cold hands forced the tight ring onto her forefinger. "There. Close your eyes."

Gbad'Wu looked uneasy. Carolle did as she was told. She could still see Gbad'Wu—the whole room in a hazy golden glow beneath her eyelids.

"Think of the men who attacked you. And say, 'Leve-me lá de volta.'"

"Leve-me lá de volta." Her vision blurred. Kneeling on Rodinger's rug, Carolle smelled the fire. Rodinger's head appeared in her hands. A flash flung her back onto her rear. She scooted out of the glowing cloud her form had become, holding Rodinger and the attention of the Filii Cinere. Firelight lit their ghostly masks. Her pulse raced, but the pain of her injuries didn't reach her here.

With Chester and Gaines, the three strangers were making their exit. "I see them," Carolle said. Her voice echoed. "And I hear rain, heavy rain." Loud as a waterfall when she looked Rodinger's way. "But it wasn't raining that night."

Sylvester's voice came from every direction. "That's the water tempting you back to the present. Don't listen to it. Silence your emotions. Taste the air on your tongue."

She managed a deep inhale against her stiff ribs.

"What can you see?" Gbad'Wu asked.

Chester. He held her focus. Carolle warily tiptoed around him to the masked strangers, half expecting them to surprise her with a swing of their maces. "Pale skin. Hateful eyes. Blue, green, and green."

Sylvester's irritated scoff bounced around the walls.

"What about their clothes?" Elanis asked. "In Racine, clothes reveal all. Needlework? Jewelry? Weapons?"

"Maces, all," Carolle answered. "Gold leaves vine about the shafts." Braving a step closer to the man nearest her, she swallowed. A shiny splatter darkened the head of his weapon. "This one, the blue-eyed one, killed Rodinger."

"That's not very helpful, girl," Sylvester said. "Give us something we can use."

Carolle studied the gap in the man's cloak. "Black jerkin, black breeches, black hose. They're all wearing it. No jewelry. But . . ." Their shoes differed. "Silver dragon wings."

"Silver dragon wings?" Elanis asked with a ring of familiarity.

"On his heels, the buckles."

Gbad'Wu asked, "Isn't the dragon restricted in Racine?"

"Yes," Elanis answered. "To Ameera's relatives. Her siblings are currently in the Warring States—not that I would suspect either. Three of her cousins, however, qualify for silver dragons. Edding departed for Oglelin with Teague last week. Yet Grand Duke Cartwright and his son are back for the winter; I saw them at the gala."

"Could both be involved?" Gbad'Wu asked.

"We shall see," Elanis answered. "What else, Carolle? What of the other two?"

Carolle continued her study with the largest of the three. "Spindleshanked, this one. There's a hole in his hose, blood and that." That wasn't much to go on. She bit her lip and bent to examine his hand. "And a large mole on his right hand. That's all I can see of him."

"How fat is he?" Sylvester asked. "More than fifty-five inches at his gut?"

"Yes? Maybe."

"Around six feet tall?" the grand diviner asked.

"Yes," Carolle answered.

"Red sprigs of a beard?"

Carolle ducked in close to the man's chest and held her breath, which returned the waterfall to her ears. A scraggly beard led down toward his throat. "I believe so. I can't see color in the shadow, mind."

"Lord Wexford," Sylvester said with certainty.

Elanis replied, "Well done."

Sylvester dismissed the compliment with a grunt. "That was the easy one. I've suspected him for some time."

Gbad'Wu asked, "What of the other, Carolle?"

Carolle checked on Chester as she went to the smaller assassin near the poster bed. "Purple, his shoes are. Dark, almost black, like."

Elanis said, "That could be anyone who was in Trône d'Argent five years ago."

"Shorter than the other two. Long brown hair. Long nails. Wait . . ." Studying the assassin's shape, Carolle confirmed her suspicion. "It's a woman! Why for would a woman want to go and bring Merith back? Draff!"

"You'd be surprised," Elanis said. "People rarely believe corruption will turn on them."

"Discuss the woman's stupidity later," Sylvester said. "Who is she?"

Boldly staring into her green eyes, Carolle squinted and backhanded the mask. Her hand passed through the memorized specter. The woman blinked. Carolle yelped and jumped back.

"What happened?" Sylvester asked.

Carolle's heart chugged but the woman remained frozen. "She moved! She blinked!"

"Good!" the grand diviner said. "Let time move forward."

"What? How?"

"Use the fire in your belly, girl! Get angry at them. But don't overdo it."

Fixating on Gaines, Carolle clenched her fists. The Filii Cinere blurred. The strangers separated from Gaines and Chester and moved toward the hallway. Carolle relaxed and inhaled deeply to halt them.

"Does she limp?" Elanis asked.

"Do assassins often bring lame partners, in your experience?" Sylvester asked with annoyance. "Less mercenary, more mage, Kimball. Now, girl, do you notice anything else about our mystery murderer?"

The woman had nearly exited the bedchamber fully. "No. Wait—yes!" Letters had been scored into the sole of her shoe. Closer to the floor, she could read the word in the dark smudge. "Yes. SHUFFLEBOTTOM is burned into her sole. Does that help?"

"Quite," Elanis answered. "It narrows things nicely enough to the Eighth Ring's cordwainer. Long brown hair. Green eyes." She sounded farther away when she said, "Shite. They're all nobles. They didn't trust their minions with this task. Could the fire have been a diversion and Rodinger's assassination their true goal?"

As the others discussed the implications, Carolle returned to Gaines. Carolle smiled smugly at the red line streaking down Gaines's face. She hadn't realized his mask had cut him when it broke. A brief conflict in Gaines's eyes vanished when he said, "No loose ends."

Their fray unfolded until her glowing form lunged. Chester's mace struck the yellow cloud in the side. They vanished. Gaines cried out. Carolle fell into the darkness, ending the spell.

When Carolle opened her eyes, the sun had gone from the window, pink with early evening light. Gbad'Wu alone remained. Seated at Carolle's side, she soaked bandages in a bowl of water that smelled distinctly of witch hazel. "Are you able to sit up?" the monk asked.

Bruised muscles protested. But with Gbad'Wu's help, Carolle managed to recline against the pillows.

Carolle scratched her forefinger. A rash encircled it where the butterfly ring had been. Strange magic.

The monk placed a saucer on Carolle's lap and offered her a lukewarm cup of tea. Carolle took a sip, then gulped it dry. Sour and bitter, the tea did little for her mood. After refilling the cup with hot tea, Gbad'Wu set it in Carolle's hands and, when convinced Carolle wouldn't spill it, returned her attention to the bowl.

Rodinger's face plagued her every time she closed her eyes. But she and Rodinger weren't the only casualties from that night. Afraid to ask, Carolle sat with her question for several minutes until she had to know. "What happened to the fire in the docks?"

Straining the bandages through her fingers, Gbad'Wu answered, "The water dragon put it out. Sadly, seven died."

"Seven?"

"This will be cold," Gbad'Wu warned. She wrapped the damp bandages about Carolle's bruised ribs. "Fortunately, our opponents were not as clever as they believe. The fools burned Lord Bernard's ship."

"The Nymphony," Carolle muttered. "Is Master Popplewell all right?"

"The engineer?" Gbad'Wu asked, tying off the final bandage. "He is fine. The Nymphony is fine too, though Queen Ameera believes it's now useless without Lord Bernard. No, they burned The Lily of the Waves."

But why? As relieved as Carolle was to hear Master Popplewell had survived, she found little joy in it. "Seven . . . Do they know who started the fire? It happened so fast; it couldn't have been the ones who attacked us."

"The Filii Cinere are plentiful. More plentiful than the queen had believed." Gbad'Wu rested her hand on Carolle's shoulder. "Do not worry. Lord Wexford and both the grand duke and his son are answering to her now. She expects to know the others involved soon."

The monk studied Carolle's unplacated reaction for a moment. She got up and returned the bowl to a cart under the window. Only then did Carolle realize Gbad'Wu wasn't wearing her usual cheerful silks. Dull black beads filled the necklace over her tightly bound black linens. Through the window, Gbad'Wu studied the sky.

"What's wrong?" Carolle asked.

"The Filii Cinere I have encountered in the past were simple. Dangerous, oui, yet mere nobles with a thirst for power." She turned from the window with a bundle of white linen in her arms. "Never mind me. If we have captured a cousin of the queen, we have surely reached the top of their coterie."

Returning to the bedside with the bundle, Gbad'Wu said, "Elanis and Sylvester hunt for clues to the mystery noblewoman in the Eighth Ring. Now that you are awake, I will join them. Before I go, I want to give you something to think over. A path forward.

"The grand diviner is working to mend your body, but he cannot mend your spirit." Gbad'Wu's kind eyes went to the white linen in her hands. "I'm familiar with the danger the Filii Cinere present. However, they are a distraction from Cyr's true woes. The world needs its balance restored. I welcome you to join the Mount and help in that pursuit."

Carolle sipped her unsweetened drink as she pondered the strange offer. No, she'd see them dead. Balancing her cup in her fingertips, she inhaled the vapor and began constructing an inoffensive decline.

"Your past life will never be safe," Gbad'Wu said, unrolling the bundle. "This is one of the weapons you saw, is it not?" Ash smudged the linen wrapped around the scorched and broken remains of a mace.

"How?" Carolle asked.

"Elanis was in a terse mood earlier," Gbad'Wu said. "One Lord Wexford barely survived."

Setting her cup on the saucer, Carolle said, "Wish he hadn't, if I'm honest."

"As does he. He will not survive Queen Ameera." That eased Carolle a bit, which tensed the monk. She tilted her head in suspicion, draping her shoulder in black curls. "I beg you to envision the fate of men who hide in shadows and use weapons coated in gilt. Do they require someone else to lead them to the grave?" Her face gave Carolle an answer she didn't want to hear.

Gbad'Wu rewrapped the weapon. "Taking a life takes from you too, in ways you cannot see. You hurt from your loss now, but that action can only prolong your pain."

Thackeray entered the room with bread, honey, and what smelled to be chicken broth on a small platter. Bandages encased his right arm to above his elbow and bound it in a sling. "My lady, I heard voices and thought you must be hungry."

Gbad'Wu rubbed Carolle's arm and got up to go, leaving the ruined weapon where it lay. "Think on my words, Carolle. I will return in the morning."

"Your spear has been sharpened and polished," Thackeray said. "It awaits you by the tunnel entrance in the study." Gbad'Wu squeezed his good arm in thanks and departed.

Thackeray's demeanor darkened when he turned back to Carolle. "I overheard what you told the others when you woke." Silent accusation threatened violence from his wrinkled face. He set the tray down and removed something from his pocket. His hand held a shard of gray porcelain close for Carolle's examination. "I found this on the floor."

Carolle folded her arms over her bandaged ribs.

"You threw Lord Bernard's tome at the man wearing this mask. That's what broke it. I know, because I found the tome out of place and this while discarding the rug stained with Lord Bernard's blood." His nostrils flared. "Whatever your lies, you saw his face. How dare you protect them!"

"What it is, Thackeray; I didn't reveal him because I do know who two of those five cockin' murderers are. They took . . ." She felt the sadness welling up inside her, stinging her eyes, but forced it down by sheer force of will. "They've taken my life. So what you're looking at is a hag of the mist, and she's coming back from the dead to drag them under." She fixed him with as menacing a stare as she could conjure. "You keep that to yourself, man."

Thackeray appraised her words without blinking. "Well then, my lady, regard me and the endowment of this estate as at your service."

Chapter II: Healthy Retribution

Clouds hung low over the sky, obscuring the peaks across the bay and scenting the air with the threat of rain. Carolle gazed wistfully at the roof of the Royal Theatre where she had watched the fireworks with her friends. Three weeks had passed since Rodinger's death. Three weeks since she'd known enough serenity to think of anything beyond a vicious constant: Gaines and Chester. With Grand Diviner Sylvester's final treatment looming, she'd deliver her requital tonight.

Thackeray entered her peripheral vision and rested his wounded arm on the balustrade.

Carolle asked, "What happens to you tomorrow?"

"I receive a new lord and master," he answered. "With the estate, so go I."

"And you're all right with that, are you?"

His lips thinned as his mind turned over her question. "To be fair, I trust Her Majesty to fill this estate with a worthy master. With luck, they'll agree to overlook my lameness until I have fully healed."

She refrained from asking what other outcomes may come his way. Their focus needed to be on tonight.

As if reading her thoughts, he opened his palm to reveal six thin darts. Carolle scooped them up and ignored the mattress hidden at the far end of the balcony, waiting for her practice with the blowpipe. Thackeray went back to brushing pigeon droppings from the balustrade.

Carolle took a few steps and squared herself with the mattress, not that a blowpipe would be of use at that range. "Have you heard from your friend? Inglewood, was it? The one tracking Chester?"

The brush's scratching bristles paused. She looked back at Thackeray. He resumed his chore and answered, "Never mind that, Lady Ysbryd. They shall find him."

"Carolle," she corrected. "Do I need to tap you with a fan to get you to stop calling me that?"

Thackeray laughed for the first time she had heard—not raspy at all, the kind of laugh that hit three notes—and carried on with a large smile. "Beg your pardon, my lady. It simply wouldn't do any good."

The blowpipe felt strange in her grasp, but then, so had a bow the first time she'd taken it up. Running her thumb over the engraved frogs in the length of hollow black wood, Carolle asked, "Why for are there frogs on this?"

"Lord Bernard asked Lord Swinton the same question, my lady. He said the Dessrini tribes use poison from venomous frogs to coat their darts. Can you imagine? Remarkable, the things one never considers."

The latch to the archway's door sprang open. Thackeray grabbed the blowpipe from Carolle and tucked it behind his bandages.

"Gormless fool," Elanis's voice echoed from inside the High House. The mage wandered through the archway with Gbad'Wu. "If you ask me, he's going to drag us all to an early grave. I understand the need for leverage with the duke of Ghest's cooperation off the table, but voluntarily entering the Cloud to find it? I may need Veen's help to pull Teague back from the ledge."

"I would be happy to deliver that message for you," Gbad'Wu said. She flung Carolle a speaking glance. "I expect to be traveling home soon." The monk had yet to accept Carolle's refusals to join her order, no matter how loud or frequent. "Now that the last of Lord Bernard's attackers is dead."

"What?" Carolle asked, caught between her excitement and fear the woman might have revealed Chester and Gaines. "You found her?"

"They found her," Elanis answered, "to eliminate our trail. Made it appear Lady Hadleigh had flung herself from her balcony."

"Do you know who 'they' are?" Carolle asked.

The mage adopted a sour voice. "That, we're still working on. Ameera isn't convinced of her husband's innocence."

"Well, tomato bisque with Alabonian toast," Thackeray said to Carolle. "Will you ladies be staying for a midday meal?"

"We'll be dining with Ameera today," Elanis answered. "Thank you, Thackeray."

Thackeray stooped and went inside.

Gbad'Wu ceased her pointed stare at Carolle and slumped for Elanis's sake. "More salmon. The same thing we ate yesterday, and the week before that; the woman eats nothing else." As diminutive as Gbad'Wu was, she loved her food.

"Carolle," Elanis said, "the grand diviner is ready for your treatment."

Downstairs in Rodinger's bedchamber, the grand diviner pestled away at a side table while Omelet anxiously waited with a small stone held in her beak. An enameled white pot held three wilted frost lilies next to his mortar.

"You brought me flowers?" Carolle asked.

Confused, Sylvester sneered until he noticed the frost lilies and grunted away the notion. He took the stone from Omelet and coated it in the poultice he'd ground. "I suppose I do owe you," he said. "This experimental magic has never been used to mend bones. You've proved to be an excellent subject. Still not convinced it should be used as a cure for caries, however."

Carolle lay on Rodinger's bed. She raised the abundant green velvet tunic she had borrowed from Rodinger's closets to below her bosom. Sylvester reached up her right side and pressed the scummy stone firmly to her ribs. She winced habitually but her bruises had healed. He cast his spell.

Sylvester's cold fingers probed her bones even after she resumed breathing. He grunted a curious note and stood upright. His eyes roamed over her, as did Omelet's.

"You don't owe me, actually," Carolle said. "Gbad'Wu insists I'd be dead if it weren't for your queer magics. Ta."

The slender mage squinted skeptically. "Well . . ." He glided out of the room without saying another word. His owl never looked back.

Gbad'Wu came in wearing a near-audible disdain for the man. "We are leaving. Do you require anything? Some clothing suitable for our voyage to the Asdales?"

Groaning, Carolle shuffled off the bed. "I told you I'm not going." The monk's set jaw turned to follow Carolle's walk to the side table. "Go on to your feast in the castle, then. You're setting my skin aquiver, man. I'm beginning to think you're a spellbreaker, you are. All quiet, wearing your thoughts in your eyes."

"The same could be said for you," Gbad'Wu replied. "Tomorrow, the mourning period ends; this House will be given to someone loyal to the throne. Where will you go? You cannot stay in Trône d'Argent, or you risk the queen being caught in a lie, which will end worse for you than for her. What keeps you here?"

"Nothing," Carolle said sharply. "Nothing keeps me here, all right? But what does it matter? Maybe I'm not as broken as you think I am." She picked up a linen towel and wiped away the residue of Sylvester's spell.

"Have you even cried?" Gbad'Wu asked.

Carolle didn't play into the question.

"No, you live for the kill," the monk said.

Carolle spun.

If Gbad'Wu suspected she knew the identity of more Filii Cinere, it didn't affect her sincerity. "Resist that temptation, Carolle. The queen will see to the Filii Cinere. I plead on your behalf."

Stolid, Carolle stood her ground.

"You do not see your potential beyond the decay of your dreams. I understand how difficult that can be. Yet I refuse to let you sacrifice yourself—"

"Really kind what you're trying to do for me," Carolle interrupted. "It is. But I do take care of myself. Maybe I'll go back to Patevia and pick up my bow. I did well as a footpad, until I got caught." The monk's glower didn't fade. Carolle verged on burning a bridge.

While the public execution of the captured Filii Cinere by way of ant infestation appeased Carolle, especially upon hearing how Grand Duke Cartwright's had been drawn out by the queen's spells, Queen Ameera's inquisition hadn't turned out Gaines or Chester over the past three weeks. Carolle wouldn't chance their escape and certainly couldn't confess their involvement now.

Thackeray entered with Carolle's meal. Gbad'Wu inhaled deeply as he passed with the bisque and cheesy toast. "If you wish," he said, "I could set some aside for later, Lady Gbad'Wu."

"No, merci. I moved my things back to the Tower's guest quarters this morning." She eyed Carolle expectantly. "And am departing at midday tomorrow, which compels me to state this: whatever you two are concocting is dangerous to yourselves and to the queen's agenda." To Thackeray's innocent reaction, she said, "Your sneaky looks. Your sudden silences. I recognize a folie à deux."

"A madness shared by two?" Thackeray asked.

"Careful, Thackeray," Carolle said, letting her tunic fall and placing the towel on the table. "She'll haul you off to the Asdales, man."

"Perhaps I should!" the monk said.

Omelet swooped in to perch on the blue upholstered chair near the fireplace and released a harsh scream at Gbad'Wu.

"He has no patience!" she yelled through the hallway. A grimace of distaste twisted the monk's mouth, first for Thackeray, then for Carolle. She stormed out more silently than Carolle had ever seen anyone manage in that mood. The owl followed.

Carolle helped Thackeray clear the mess the grand diviner had forgotten. He took the mortar and pestle from her hands and nodded to the food. "Please eat."

Folding over a piece of cheesy toast, Carolle dunked it into the tomato bisque. She took a bite and chewed while watching him work. "Did you leave the flowers?"

Thackeray brushed his hand on his doublet and centered the lilies on the table. "Yes. Lord Bernard's favorite." She froze mid chew when he clenched the stems and jerked the roots free of the soil. With a knife, he sliced the roots and dropped the trimmings into the mortar. "It is only fitting they help avenge him with their poison."

Glancing at the door, Carolle asked at a near whisper, "It won't kill them, will it? I don't want to give them a sudden death, mind."

"The toxin only paralyzes, my lady," he replied, just as quietly.

She resumed eating as he juiced the stems into the mortar. "Hey, now, don't use your arm so much. You heard what the physician said."

"Very well," Thackeray agreed. His left arm worked the pestle, crushing the toxin and roots together. "May I ask your intentions for the second mask of King Vendral, my lady?"

Carolle wiped the sweet bisque from her lips with a cotton napkin and said, "A distraction in case Gbad'Wu and the others are closing in on our marks."

Thackeray crushed the poisoned mixture violently. Regardless, his voice was calm as he asked, "Where shall I have it delivered?"

"I've written it out," she answered. "One moment."

Anxious to test Sylvester's success for herself, Carolle went to Rodinger's long corridor of closets. She stretched. Rising to the balls of her bare feet on the parquet floor, the simple elevé refocused her balance. Alternating hops brought her farther past the dressing rooms and last year's accoutrements. Glissades, a pas de chat, and a saut de chat got her down most of the hallway. Not perfectly. But the stiffness would subside in a few hours. She opted for a grand jeté to leap the rest of the way to the daylight spilling out of Rodinger's private gallery. Her right arm was beset by a tremor after the exertion. Unacceptable.

If she really wanted to test herself, and she must, her practice called for a dress rehearsal. On the settee in Rodinger's studio, the leather armor Thackeray had commissioned lay in order. He had insisted on the most expensive cuir-bouilli; a soft camlet lining; and, in true Racinian fashion, that the whole outfit match the leather boots in both ivy design and umber color. Unfortunately, enchantments within the purchasing grasp of High Houses required too long for them to wait, not that Thackeray wished to go through the Tower's approval process, regardless.

The many phases of Lady Madeline and Lady Rose watched Carolle change from about the room. "I'll be needing your strength tonight, ladies," she said, fastening the leather vambrace over her right forearm.

Taking up the letter she had penned for the distraction, she viewed Rodinger's easel. "Fool," Carolle said to the canvas of the incomplete work, a sketch of her laughing at Lake Sabine. Only her dress and the leaves had been painted, in that yellow.

Carolle returned to the hallway. Surprisingly, the return test fared better. Her leathers no longer hindered nor pinched.

When she entered the bedchamber, Thackeray asked, "Do your garments require any further tailoring?"

"No, dim diolch."

He traded her the slim leather case of darts for the letter. She affixed the case to her belt. "All six darts have been treated, my lady. Please, aim carefully."

Upon reading the address on the parchment, Thackeray tilted his head forward and gave her that look a bampi gives his grandchildren when he catches them about to do something naughty. "Anything else?"

"Not right now," she answered. "More practice, mind."

After a couple of hours of loosening up in her armor, Carolle removed her boots. She poured heat back into her cup and strolled upstairs to the balcony. An icy drizzle held her back from the balustrade. She drank and pined for the theatre until she no longer felt her toes and the sky had gone dark with an early eve of winter.

Returning to Rodinger's bedchamber, she curled into the blue armchair with her thoughts and let the fire thaw her feet.

Thackeray scraped a sturdy short sword they had found in the study against a whetstone. "A message arrived while you were outside. Gaines and Fellows have departed on time for the Orchestral Hall. You may wish to get ready."

Carolle got up and examined the items lying on the bed. Her nerves began to work against her as she slid on her boots. She willingly summoned the look of betrayal on Rodinger's face to burn her jitters away. Thackeray presented the short sword as she worked her boot's buckle.

"Lady Ysbryd . . ." His mouth hung open, hesitant to say something. "A good servant knows his lord's desires before he knows them himself. There is nothing Lord Bernard would withhold from you." He searched her eyes. His face saddened. "With the exception of danger for his sake. I lied to you earlier; they found my friend Inglewood. They found half of him in the bay, my lady."

Stunned, Carolle got to her feet but had no clue what to say. His pride gone, Thackeray appeared shrunken and shriveled. She gripped his shoulders to strengthen him.

"I'm sorry I didn't tell you earlier," he said. "Part of me didn't want to talk you out of our plan. Yet you need to know I would not think less of you should you forgo it all and return with Lady Gbad'Wu to the monastery."

Carolle refused to quail and removed the sword from his hands.

"Steady, Thackeray. I'm committed to this. They're not getting away with it. For Inglewood too, all right?"

"Of course."

Carolle slid the sword into her pack and collected the gray cloak. They ventured upstairs to Rodinger's study, where Thackeray dug around in the desk drawers. She could tell he was debating another attempt to talk her out of it; she felt his pensive expression on her while she perused the wares on the shelves.

Thackeray removed a brown stone, brought it to her, and placed it in her palm. Smooth, except for some worn etchings, it bewildered her. "Here we are," he said. His aged thumb pressed hers to the center of the carvings. The markings shone with an orange glow to fill the dwarven insignia. "This shall provide you with enough light to see in the tunnels. Remove your thumb and . . ." The light extinguished.

"There is one more way I can help you," he said, fishing around in his pocket. His knobby fingers pulled free a strip of faded red cloth. "Magic is not something many possess these days, yet this heirloom has given me the strength of three men in the past. Though I never learnt of its origin, I like to believe it was torn from Braxton's tunic." Carolle grinned at the idea of Thackeray following the god of bravery, whom most called the god of brashness. He smiled bashfully and tied the scrap around her right wrist. "Do not mock this old fool, my lady. My father put the notion in my head when he gave it to me."

"Thackeray, this means a lot to me. Really. Diolch yn fawr." She hugged him.

"You are very welcome, Lady Ysbryd. Be safe. Be thorough." They shared a kindred agony in their smiles.

Thackeray collected her mask of King Vendral. As he settled it onto her head, she clamped her fingers and recited, "Three tunnels down, one left, five down, two right."

"To the alleyway, yes."

She switched hands. "Then one right, four down, two right."

"To the west entrance of the queen's wardrobe. I've paid the guards to take a break until dawn, for their own safety. Be sure to leave your mask in place until you're inside." He stepped back and refused to look at the mask for more than a second.

"Why for?"

"Because you are dead, my lady."

"Right."

"Would you like to take Lord Bernard's map?"

Carolle shook her head. "I've got it."

Thackeray pulled forward the golden frame, entered the tunnel, and unlocked the gate of iron bars he had had installed to replace the deceased guards Carolle thankfully hadn't seen the night of the attack. While he rattled the lock, she untied his heirloom. Thackeray returned and helped her don the gray woolen cloak. Carolle ignored the hint of fear in his shaky lips as he raised her hood. She blew him a kiss to distract from her left hand dropping his heirloom onto the chessboard. He had lost enough, and she didn't expect to return.

With mounting dread, Carolle breached the dank darkness. Though Gbad'Wu and Elanis had already swept the passages beyond, panic knocked at Carolle's chest with the locking of the gate behind her. Her thumb pressed against the dwarven stone, illuminating the ancient Creb tunnels beneath Trône d'Argent.

The musty passages weren't of dwarven construction; the stonework hadn't fully survived the test of time. Roots, draining water, and rats had penetrated both the ceilings and the walls. "No spiders, please," Carolle whispered. "And no godsforsaken Filii Cinere."

Down several ladders and a staircase, she came to the rough-dressed stone expansion Thackeray said Rodinger had been commissioning for years. Thus began her carefully memorized directions. After the last turn, Carolle ascended an inset ladder to the sewer beneath the Theatre District. Another climb put her in an alley across from the black-bricked Orchestral Hall, exactly as Thackeray said it would.

She stowed the dwarven stone in her pack and fished out the letter detailing instructions for Gaines. Then, with her cloak gathered tightly about her, she waited for her prey in the shadows and winter drizzle.

Carriages queued in front of the hall, anticipating the end of the performance. Carolle's stomach churned. Upon hearing applause, she wanted little else than to be free of that mask, to feel the fresh, cool air on her face. Instead, she retrieved the short sword and recalled Rodinger's anguished expression for Grand Duke Cartwright's lie. She squeezed the hilt of the sword.

Nobles emerged slowly at first but soon swarmed the steps. Many raced for their carriages to preserve their foolish wigs and hairstyles. There he was! In pastel yellow, the bastard. And his rib-bashing beast in tow. Carolle's stomach knotted. "Luce?"

Lucille beamed, affixed to Chester's arm as they scurried down the steps.

Someone had informed Gaines of the Nymphony, forcing Carolle into a corner. Could Lucille have succumbed to the coin after all? Did she know what her beloved Chester had done? Contrary to her doubts, sickness wormed its way through Carolle, then lit her on fire.

In the street's lamplight, Carolle stuck her fingers under her mask and whistled. Several people heard but only Gaines balked. He didn't break his line of sight to her mask as he descended. When the carriages on the street blocked his view of her, Carolle dropped the letter and ran to the sewer. She didn't stop running until she hid behind a corner.

For several minutes, she waited, sword in hand, for him to follow, for him to disavow his instructions and the delivered threat. She and Thackeray didn't know how the Filii Cinere communicated. They had to risk luring him out with this charade.

Convinced Gaines wasn't coming after her, Carolle lit her surroundings in the orange light and began counting passageways on her way to the queen's wardrobe. Her hopes now hinged on ample time to set her trap. And, of course, that they had threatened him with the right bait.

Chapter 12: The Royal Wardrobe

The tunnel deposited Carolle across the vacant alley from the queen's marble behemoth of a wardrobe and directly into the guards' line of sight. "Steady," Carolle whispered to herself, feeling the armed sentries' eyes on her.

"I don't know about you, Weathers," one robust guard said to the other, "but I could use a drink." True to Thackeray's word, they vacated the entrance.

Carolle waited until they rounded the corner of the next alley and she hurried inside. Built over three city blocks, the monarchy's wardrobe had been laid out in aisles of actual wardrobes and relics beneath the hundred-foot ceiling. Amid the smell of old fabric and wood, enchanted pedestals held up smaller mementos and cast yellow light down the blue-and-white carpeted paths. Thackeray had told her each aisle contained one year of the ruler's life.

Overwhelmed by the size, Carolle spun on the carpets, wondering where Ameera's life began. Selecting an aisle, she struck off, scouting for an indication of where in time she stood.

A tapestry hung between two antique banner posts. In dark thread, King Clyde signed a treaty with the antler-helmeted Barundal tribe, which he infamously betrayed later. Green thread dated the event: 646.

Carolle dashed to the next aisle. No signs to guide her there, she ran on another seventeen years.

Sprinting down the aisle for either year 628 or year 664, she came upon a steel and glass case. Double sleeves of green and blue relayed the queen mother's Patevian roots while the white needlework of fleurs-de-lis foretold the bride's new loyalties to the empire. "Six sixty-four," Carolle said.

The grand wedding display preserved all of the royals' garb behind glass, even those of the queen's twins from a previous marriage. No relic too large, the bridal carriage had been parked at the end of the case. Magnificent, but the wrong year for Carolle.

Racing forward in time, she counted off the years to the queen's coronation. "Six eighty-one," she whispered. "Six eighty-two."

The silver-laden coronation carriage sat halfway through the year. Carolle dropped her pack next to it and removed her mask. She wiped her clammy face on her gray grogram cloak, then stripped it off, too. Time to see if Thackeray's friends had been successful.

Across the aisle, Carolle opened a creaking whitewood wardrobe and released the stench of urine overwhelming the nobleman's bath powder. Beneath several dresses of Queen Ameera's attendants, the elder Lord Gaines lay bound, soiled, and unconscious. She hauled him out onto the carpets. The fall woke him, setting him into a squirming tantrum. He tried to scream through his gag.

The fire in his eyes reignited hers. She grinned down on her captive. "How did you get here?" she asked. "Is that what you're wondering? How dare this Patevian stand here while you're restrained? Is that it?" She opened the worked leather case of darts on her belt. "Well, maybe those people you like to stand on, Lord Gaines, aren't as weak or as invisible as you treat them. Impressed, I am, if I'm honest. I didn't realize the real power of Trône d'Argent was held by the help."

Carolle jabbed one of the poisoned quills into Lord Gaines's arm. "What it is, Lord Gaines, I'm supposed to be asking if you're part of the Filii Cinere."

The man froze, terrified, which was more justification than her animosity required.

"Truth is, I don't much care. Probably because your son tried to kill me. I can't imagine a good man could rear a son who'd do a thing like that. Can you?"

The whites of the man's eyes remained exposed as she propped him up against the wardrobe. "Now, don't worry about the poison. It won't kill you. It shouldn't." She gripped his jerkin in her fists.

Struggling with his dead weight, Carolle almost cursed herself for leaving Thackeray's heirloom behind. She eventually managed to get the man propped up against one of the enchanted pedestals holding a gaudy garnet brooch. The pedestal's light should make him easier to spot from both ends of the aisle. After retrieving her mask of King Vendral, she set it over his face. His eyes protested behind it.

Their stratagem had called for her to lie in wait inside the carriage with her blowpipe at the ready. However, seeing it now, Carolle decided to alter the plan. Envisioning the possibility of getting trapped inside made her skin crawl. She'd much prefer the tops of the wardrobes.

Tossing her pack up, she climbed the carriage and leaped over. Nice and deep, the back-to-back wardrobes of the two aisles gave her enough room to lie in wait.

Carolle loaded a dart, removed the short sword from her pack, and flattened herself. Silent as a snake in water, she waited.

Within minutes, her patience waned. It had to be close to midnight. The letter said they had to arrive by then to save Lord Gaines. Perhaps she had misjudged the relationship between the father and son.

"Down here," a man's voice whispered.

The dundun returned to Carolle's chest. Easing the pipe into place, she lay low. Pins and needles ran along her arms. For Rodinger, for Carolle Ysbryd, she focused.

Chester appeared first, concealed in his Filii Cinere garb. He knelt by Lord Gaines. "He's alive." Then he pocketed the sparkling garnet brooch.

"Pick him up," Gaines ordered from behind his mask, approaching with more caution. He avoided getting too close to the wardrobes as though he suspected someone would jump out of one at any moment. Carolle ducked until he said, "Whoever that man was, he wasn't part of our coterie."

Debating between her two targets, Carolle's mind recommended brawny Chester, but acrid anger demanded Gaines.

Chester's broad shoulders rose with Lord Gaines. Carolle inhaled deeply and put her mouth to the pipe. A puff sent Gaines's hand to his shoulder. He moaned and collapsed. Chester dropped Lord Gaines and immediately looked to the carriage.

Carolle loaded another dart, aimed, and blew. It plinked into Chester's mask. He ripped it off. His deep-set eyes found her. Chester dashed to the carriage and climbed. Her next dart missed when he leaped to the tops of the wardrobes.

Rising with the short sword in hand, Carolle faced her would-be killer. Chester's posture stiffened. "You?" He drew two daggers. So much for his bringing his bloody mace. He charged. An anger to match her own bellowed out with his yell.

She ducked one swipe and leaped back from another. Regaining some ground with a low kick and an upward slash, Carolle attempted to force him back to the edge.

Chester searched behind himself and hunkered down. Perhaps he wasn't as dumb as she believed. His daggers blocked her thrusts, one after another. He confidently shuffled close. Little by little, Carolle gave ground until she reached her pack and refused to give more.

Flipping the dagger in his right hand, Chester grinned. "One less flea," he said, and threw the blade.

She dodged it, but not his tackle. The impact knocked the sword from her hand and the air from her lungs. His hands clamped down on her throat. Choking, she pressed her head away from his sneer.

"I know the truth of you. Just another whore like your 'mam.' Screwing people to get your coin." He punched her.

She tasted the iron in her blood. Black flecks bordered her vision. She'd been there before. Oddly, the thought comforted her. Her right hand went to the dart case on her belt, but Chester pinned it under his knee. She quit fighting to free her arm and hunted with the other. Her fingers found her pack and something hard. All the strength she could muster smashed the dwarven stone against Chester's skull.

He fell over the edge, but caught her arm and jerked. Carolle's back hit the carpets hard. She forced herself up and scrambled onto her feet.

Blood trickled from Chester's ear. He raised her short sword in his hand. "You cannot win. Your kind never wins." Grimacing at the blood that came away on his hand, he swayed. Carolle kicked at his sword arm but missed when he collapsed with his hand to his ear.

Stretching against the wardrobe, Carolle found the blowpipe. She dropped a dart inside. Seething anger lured her closer to Lucille's suitor. Her fingers pinched her last dart. She tiptoed around him toward the short sword. In a fluid lunge, she drove the dart into his arm and stole the blade.

Now for her vengeance. While Grand Duke Cartwright had misled Rodinger, Gaines had brought her into this mess in the first place. Carolle tore off Gaines's mask. "You cost me everything! You wrecked my life!"

His green eyes struggled to stay open. "I . . . I tried to save you, Carolle." His gaze went to her raised sword. "I did! I promise . . . I told them the wrong ship, didn't I?"

Her blade lowered to her side but rose again. "You gave your goon the order to kill me, Barimor Gaines."

Gaines sobbed. "I know. I am sorry." He croaked and whimpered.

Uncomfortable with the display, Carolle refused to believe his words to be anything more than an attempt to save himself. "You could have fought them! I would have stood with you." She pointed the tip of the short sword at Chester. "That twpsyn would have stood with you."

"I wouldn't help that idiot, bitch!" Chester said, attempting to rise from the floor. His poisoned body fought against him. Carolle mercilessly heeled his ribs, dropping him flat to the carpets. The edge of her sword met the sweat on his throat. It slid deeply across his neck with little hesitation. Blood streamed into the expensive carpets.

Her mind consumed by rage, she knelt next to Gaines.

"Carolle . . . Carolle . . . please. Run! We didn't come into your trap alone."

At the west end of the aisle, five Filii Cinere waited with their weapons ready. Six more masks watched from the east. Carolle rose, ready to climb the carriage again, but flinched when Gbad'Wu said, "Neither did she."

Atop the wardrobes, the monk raised her spear into the air. Sylvester's barn owl soared over and screeched. Panicked shouts erupted from the east end of the aisle, where a purple haze enveloped the six men. They choked on the spell and fell.

Appearing out of the air near Lord Gaines, Elanis raced forward and slung a pouch westward at the Filii Cinere. "Na kamen i da odite!" Powder burst from the pouch in a pink cloud. Before it reached its target, however, the cloud parted and disappeared.

Standing with the Filii Cinere, a brunette woman in rags lowered her arms. Arcs of fire leaped between her hands.

"Shite!" Elanis said. "They've collared a magus!" She ran past Carolle. "Go! Run!"

Gbad'Wu kept pace atop the wardrobes as they raced toward the dissipating purple haze. Green-scaled creatures crawled out from beneath the gray cloaks. Goblins? The spell had turned the men into goblins? The grand diviner thwacked one in the head with his silver staff before noticing Carolle and Elanis dashing at him.

An explosion flung Carolle forward to the carpets. She rolled over and grabbed her sword. Ten feet away, fire climbed the wardrobes. Flames consumed Gaines, his father, and the body of Chester Fellows. "No!" she yelled.

Whizzes, whistles, and bone-shaking booms got Carolle on her feet again. A basket of unused fireworks spread the blaze, showering the aisle in white sparks.

Uncannily calm now, Elanis said, "They've collared a magus, Grand Diviner."

Squinting down on her, Sylvester thought and whacked another goblin with his staff. "Very well. I'll deal with it. Gather these for the queen's inquisition."

Carolle kicked away one of the pik-sized goblins. She had no interest in an inquisition. Her vengeance had been stolen from her. "There are five Filii Cinere over by there."

Sylvester's frosty glare stalled her. "The monk shall see to them." He grabbed Carolle's arm and shoved her back into the acrid stench of his spell hanging in the air. "Do not let them bite you. They're venomous in this form."

The grand diviner drifted down the smoking aisle where the magus splayed her fingers at Omelet. Lightning scattered around the owl until she flew out of sight. Sylvester opened a tiny compartment in his staff, held it out, and mumbled something. Wind stirred his robes before the flames died.

Something crunched behind Carolle. A goblin crumpled under the Filii Cinere's mace in Elanis's hands. "The spell wears off," Elanis said. "Are you going to help? There are three more somewhere."

Kicking at the cloaks, Carolle watched the magi and ground her teeth. Someone had to pay. This was her fight! She wouldn't sit it out.

Beyond the posturing magi, a spear jabbed at the men in gray cloaks. Carolle hared off. Elanis called after her, but Carolle didn't slow her pace down year 683. Veering away from the sparks of the magi battle, she let her fury boil over.

Gbad'Wu had felled two of the Filii Cinere. The blunt end of her spear cracked into a mask's nose. Crying out, the gray-cloaked woman fell.

She cried louder when Gbad'Wu dodged an arcing sword and thrust her spear into the woman's knee. With a quick leap, the monk unmasked another Filii Cinere. She landed hard on his calf.

Taking advantage of the chaos, Carolle pattered back down 682 behind the Filii Cinere magus. Trapped by an unseen force, a rainbow of colorful gases swirled between the magus and Sylvester. The magi had warded themselves well enough that lightning struck only their surroundings.

Carolle crept closer at first, but purple flares blinded her the more she saw of the battle. For Rodinger, for herself, she sprinted down the singed carpets.

"Carolle, no!" Gbad'Wu yelled.

The magus turned as Carolle leaped, her sword poised. Without mercy, the blade stabbed through the magus's belly. Carolle wrenched her sword free.

Wide-eyed, the magus gurgled. A girl. Just a girl. Starved. Frail, like Braith. Mathanas's forgiving smile crossed the magus's lips briefly. She fell forward.

Confused at first, the grand diviner dismissed the spells the girl's fallen wards had loosed. He cautiously approached and rolled the magus over.

Standing away from the death in the girl's eyes, Carolle shuddered. She dropped her blade. Gbad'Wu picked it up. "She was innocent," the monk said. "The one who put that collar around her throat forced her to fight us."

"Untenable, yes," Sylvester said, kneeling at the girl's side. "You saved her the pain of healing, however." Carolle watched in a daze as he closed her eyelids. Sylvester removed the band of leather from around her throat. "Though her strength would have compensated for the challenge of rehabilitation." He rubbed the florid marks on the girl's arms. "The Speaker carved wards into her skin. Clever."

His owl screeched from the wardrobe above him. The grand diviner put his fingertip to his lips and regarded the girl. "Wait, yes. Yes, you're correct. Nettles. Dana Nettles. She's one of ours." He throttled his staff and used it to stand. "They have their nasty fingers in my Tower!"

Elanis murmured a lamentation behind him. "Well, someone help me find the last two goblins. Then we shall set our traps for the traitors."

"Think, Mage Kimball!" the grand diviner shouted. He clicked his tongue, which compelled Omelet to flight. "Omelet can hunt the goblins. There's a Speaker nearby. A Speaker I intend to question." He slid open another groove in his staff, pressed the collar against it, and shouted, "Oclinar festia'na!"

His words hurled the coronation carriage into the air. It crashed down a few years over, jolting Carolle back into the moment. The spell bored through the aisles, flinging furniture and gowns until a man stood in the clearing. Gbad'Wu's outstretched arm forced Carolle from his line of sight. The monk and Elanis set off to flank the Speaker. Sylvester strode directly toward him.

Carolle ran. Dana Nettles's eyes haunted her. She fled through the years and escaped the spellcasters' rumbling battle. Outside, she nearly tripped, stumbling to a sudden halt.

Soldiers raised their shields and readied their broadswords. Pikemen completed the ends of the arc, sealing off her escape. Queen Ameera moved a fleur-de-lis shield edged in shock crystals aside. "We do not see her," she announced. Resuming a stance at attention, the soldiers pretended to see only the entrance. The queen came to her, jowls raised, fan choked closed. Carolle avoided the queen's fury with a curtsy, which felt strange in armor, almost insincere.

"Spirit," the queen said, her voice sharp, "why have you selected my wardrobe for your trap?"

Muddled, Carolle answered, "Thackeray said—" Too late to take it back, she carried on, "He said you had the power to make it disappear. To make the scandal disappear, Your Majesty."

Unreadable, the queen studied her. "I see. In his wisdom, did he honestly believe he could bribe my guards without my knowledge?"

"Please," Carolle said. "He—we only wanted justice for Rodinger."

Queen Ameera raised her voice. "What precisely do you think I have been doing? While we have followed every thread attached to the Filii Cinere—no matter how miniscule—you have actively concealed them from us!"

Carolle crossed her arms over her midriff to still her shaking. "I'm sorry."

Flowing gracefully around Carolle toward the entrance, the queen asked, "Have they detained the traitors, Gbad'Wu?"

"Oui, Your Majesty," the monk answered. Carolle didn't turn to face Gbad'Wu. "Sylvester and Elanis have subdued the Speaker. They question him now."

"Speaker?" Queen Ameera asked. Her gown rustled as she raced to the entrance. The guards rushed after her. Carolle swam through them to avoid Gbad'Wu but didn't get far.

"I won't ask again," Gbad'Wu called out to her.

Pained by the hammering question left in all of this madness and that Gbad'Wu still believed her worth saving, Carolle fought to maintain her poise. She wiped her nose and shuddered at the possibility Lucille may have betrayed her. "I understand. And I'm sorry." Carolle walked on.

Lucille couldn't be involved. She wouldn't betray her like this. And yet Carolle had to be certain. "I've got to see the dragon."

Chapter 13: The Water Dragon

The dragon's guard inspected Carolle's silver drop necklace. "You're bleeding," he said and pulled a clean kerchief from beneath his pauldron.

Carolle pressed it to her stinging lip, now realizing why Rumer had been staring at her when she'd retrieved the necklace and purse. "Diolch."

"One of the Dragoneers' own, then?" the guard asked. "Harishnu cannot get enough of you Patevians." He stepped aside to bid Carolle entry to the den.

Her thoughts clung to suspicions, with every raw fiber of her being hoping against what she had begun to accept as true. Lucille had betrayed her. Someone had told Gaines about the Nymphony before he'd coerced it out of her.

Numb from more than the cold, Carolle chose right at a fork in the passageway, correctly assuming each path led to the water dragon's indoor lake. Plucked harp strings beckoned her into the sea air of the cavernous marble, lapis, and azurite den.

Clinging to the marble edge of the lake with his second pair of front legs, the serpentine dragon spotted Carolle at the top of the stairs. His two robed servants grew quiet near the edge beneath him. Harishnu bobbed and watched Carolle descend the scalloped steps. Bending his neck to scratch his scraggly white beard with a talon, the dragon said to his servants, "Do as I've asked." The boom in his voice echoed. "Merahme, a break, please."

The harpist silenced the golden instrument between the staircases. As she ascended the staircase on the far side of the room, Harishnu's men collected the dragon's ear from Carolle on their way out.

Sea-green fins crested Harishnu's large head and all the way down his back. He sniffed in Carolle's direction. The water dragon flopped back into his pool with a graceless splash and dived deep out of sight.

Carolle approached the water's edge on the marble floor and peered into the dark waves. "Please tell me . . ." Her strength waned. Did she want to know? She could pretend Lucille was innocent. The guilt of betraying Rodinger stung too deeply. She raised her voice. "Tell me—"

Rising above Carolle, Harishnu clutched the marble again and held himself forward while paddling with his hind four legs. "You are in quite the state, Carolle Graean." A gentle rumble in his words had her second-guessing herself again. His fogging breath chilled her face as it fell over her.

"I've got a question for you, Master Harishnu."

The dragon tilted his head and sank lower into the lake. His bearded chin settled on the marble. "My dear, Lucille Morgan suspected those now-charred corpses of murdering you. She aimed to avenge you this very eve."

Carolle clapped her hand over her heart and fell to her knees. Her wall of enmity crumbled. Weakened and huddled over on all fours, she wept. Wept for the hatred that had brought her to a horrible mistake. Wept for Rodinger. Wept for suspecting her closest friend of betrayal. Wept for the years of hard work that had led her here, to where she had to accept she had no way forward.

Dripping across the marble, Harishnu hauled himself out and lay around her. His long mouth barely opened when he said, "If you want to lean on me, you may."

She laid her face on his smooth blue scales. Reaching forward, Carolle stroked his white beard.

He brought his head closer. "She thinks of you often. Always when she dances as Elysant."

Carolle's wet cheeks lifted in a grin.

"You know," Harishnu said, "I never believed my grandmother's stories about our kin coming to this world together. And yet every Patevian who visits me smells distinctly alike and powerfully different from the other humans."

Carolle didn't know what to say to that. She pulled Gaines's purse in front of her. "I know I've asked my question and shouldn't ask—"

"No, you haven't." Carolle blinked at the dragon's interruption. "I told you the answer to your question without your asking."

"Really kind of you, that is," she said. "But I—"

"May I ask what you plan to do when you leave my den?"

"I don't know." Looking into his shiny cobalt eyes flecked with teal and amber, she said, "They're dead. The bastards . . ." She felt emptier, yet still broiled with anger at the edges. A cold, webbed paw rubbed her back. "I've got no plan. I have no way to make it right. Not truly."

Harishnu withdrew himself and slunk into the water. It churned. Carolle got up and went to the choppy lake, now lapping the edge at her feet. In the deep, the water dragon's scales reflected a silvery light. He wound himself around in patterns of figure eights and full circles. The frothing waves blocked Carolle's view.

Harishnu's finned crown broke the surface and cut the waves as he swam forward. He rose to clutch the side of the lake again. "The past and future brush the present. Allow me to help as best I can by revealing the paths open to you."

Stepping out of his breath, she urged him on with a solemn nod.

"There are avenues around your broken heart," he said. "One I must state should not be taken, though it calls to you. Your troupe performs through their mourning and would welcome you back both with great joy and at great peril." The benefit to Lucille made his words nearly bearable.

Her attempted grin faded into grimness when the dragon said, "Your mother . . ." She detected his sympathy and focused on her joined fingers. "Her deathbed has found her in Deganwy on the Patevian coast. You have time to say farewell if you gain passage on the Wave Bender leaving the port in a little over an hour."

Straightening her back, Carolle urged the dragon to continue with a single shake of her head.

"The traveler, the midwife," he said. "The path to the Mount remains open to you but only if you approach it with honesty."

Carolle raised her eyebrows. "That's not what she said."

He slunk up into the air as his back legs paddled. "These are the options I see tied to your previous life. Make a decision and define your existence. Otherwise, if you wish to escape all of these, I can tell you how to avoid being seen on your way out of Trône d'Argent. The purse at your feet will be of much use in that plan."

The coins in Gaines's purse clinked when Carolle kicked it. "Have Dafydd and Madame Davies visited you?"

"No." Harishnu sank lower. "Ameera Koenig has seen to the misplacement of the droplets given to Dilys Davies and Dafydd Gallivan for fear they would ask of you. You wish this given to them?"

"Yes, to Dafydd, please," Carolle answered. He and Braith would see to Lucille's well-being without her being tempted by the coin. "Stalwart Dafydd, gentle Braith . . . they are your people. I am . . ." She shrugged. "Sorry to ask a favor. I can find another way."

Harishnu's webbed hand lurched forward to scoop up the purse with a black talon. "For the descendants of the Dragoneers, there are few favors I can deny and fewer I would." The purse splashed into the water. "I shall deliver it myself." That surprised her. "What? I do not answer to Ameera Koenig and am not contained in this den by any force other than my own desire. Do you want him to know the truth of his good fortune?"

"Never." The answer came instinctively.

The water dragon smiled like a dog. "My dear, do you ever find life will take you where it wants you to go? Or in this case, where the water guides you?"

When her mouth opened to ask what he meant, a man called, "We have returned, sire." One of Harishnu's servants held Gbad'Wu's spear and let the Creb-Daijon enter. She straightened her black bead necklace and soundlessly stepped down to Carolle's side.

"I have never been summoned by a dragon," Gbad'Wu said.

"Sadly, dear Wu of the Gbad tribe," the dragon said, "I did not invite you here for my conversation." Carolle observed the mist falling to the floor. "You, Carolle Graean." He nudged her with his finger. "Speak your penitence."

"What is this?" Gbad'Wu asked Carolle.

"I hadn't made my choice," Carolle said to the dragon.

He splayed four of his webbed hands and grinned slyly. "The water made me do it. Take your rightful path, an option not open to Elysant." Harishnu plunged into the depths as his icy breath fell over them, prickling Carolle's flushed cheeks and fogging the monk's beads.

"I'm sorry," Carolle said. "I won't lie to you, Gbad'Wu. I think behind my anger—I thought if I couldn't save Rodinger, maybe I could still save myself. It doesn't matter; I couldn't." She wiped her cheeks and cleared her throat. "I'd like to go with you if you'll still have me. But you should know I had a bigger role in this than you knew. More than I knew, really. I didn't mean to but I did. And I couldn't set it right."

The monk harbored genuine sadness in her smile. "I am sorry I could not spare you the events of tonight." She took Carolle's arm. "Come, confess your thoughts on the road. That is, if you are tired of vengeance? You will not take more lives in my company."

As they climbed the stairs, Carolle looked back to the water. Owning a sense of purpose helped. Some. "I'll do whatever I can to make it right. You have my word on that."

After Gbad'Wu retrieved her spear, they exited the dragon's den for the vacant early-morning street. Carolle's heart jumped when a shocked voice called her name.

Lucille sprinted away from the second of Harishnu's attendants. She tackled Carolle in a hug that brought them both to the ground. "Carolle! They told us you was dead." Lucille hugged her again. She pinched Carolle's hand in front of her disbelieving eyes.

Gbad'Wu laid a hand over her heart. "Take a moment," she said. Then she asked Harishnu's servant, "Can you help me send a message? It will require an escort to the Tower." They returned to the den.

Lucille's fingers prodded Carolle's face.

"I'm alive, Luce," Carolle said. "I couldn't tell you. Gaines and Chester—"

"I knew it!" Lucille said. "I mean, I thought they killed you. Or somehow, they had something to do with it. Gods, Carolle, I was going to kill them tonight. But something came up and they abandoned me at the hall." Lucille squinted at Carolle's smile. "I'm not being funny; I had the poison and everything, like."

"They tried," Carolle said. She actually felt her face brighten. "Luce, I came up. They came to find me. But they're dead now, biwt." Tears came unexpectedly and easily when Lucille blinked faster. Carolle rose. "I've got to go."

Lucille seized Carolle's arm. "What? No. No, you don't."

"The Filii Cinere will come after me—and the troupe—if I stay."

Lucille cocked her head. "Who?"

"Nobles," Carolle answered. "Bad ones."

Raising her chin, Lucille said, "Let them come for us. We'll fight them!"

"You will. Dafydd would. Braith?" That took some of the wind out of Lucille's sails. And a bit from Carolle's. Poor Dana Nettles. "We're artists now. Madame Davies did that for us. Honor her."

"No! You've gone daft. You're coming back with me, you are!"

Carolle gripped Lucille's arms and put more confidence into her voice than she felt. "Then you'll honor me, you will, Lucille Morgan. I've spent three weeks listening to the grand diviner, a mage from the Hook, and that monk over by there plotting against these draffs. They've been working the shadows against the Filii Cinere at the queen's request. Queen Ameera. A grand diviner, Luce." She gave her friend a bit of a shake. "The Filii Cinere would kill us all."

Pulling her into a cwtch, Carolle laid her head against Lucille's. "That's not my life anymore. I'll always hate them for taking it from me. But I'm glad Elysant knows you now."

Lucille moaned. "Will I get to see you again? You can't just leave forever, can you? Not now that I know you're alive."

"I'll find you. We don't have to like it, but them's the rules."

Two soldiers in dragon-embossed plate armor clanked toward Verdict Hill with Gbad'Wu's message. The monk and Harishnu's servant approached. "Master Harishnu wishes to see you now," the servant said to Lucille.

Lucille blinked at him a few times. "He wants to see me? I thought this was to see Carolle."

"Go on, then," Carolle said. Their fingers parted. "And, Luce bach, tell him I said diolch yn fawr, all right?" After one final hug, Lucille accompanied the dragon's attendant. Carolle waited until she disappeared inside.

When Carolle caught up to Gbad'Wu, the monk said, "My preference for travel is walking. However, we should get you out of Racine before too many see you." She gestured down the street to the west end of the docks and set their path.

"Gbad'Wu."

"Oui?"

"Did Thackeray tell you how to find me?"

"No." The shorter woman bumped Carolle with her shoulder. "Retaliation is not a motive original to you, Carolle. My role requires a pinch of disbelief and suspicion."

As they strolled, Carolle explained what she had done at Gaines's request. Gbad'Wu heard it all without interruption, though she paused to console Carolle twice. "I failed," Carolle said. "I didn't see the whole match." The monk raised a quizzical eyebrow. "I should've known Gaines wouldn't come with just Chester Fellows."

"In time, you will see this evening was not a complete loss. You cannot confess to Rodinger, yet Queen Ameera shone with approval for so many to put to the question. I thought she might resurrect Carolle Ysbryd to offer thanks."

"Carolle Ysbryd," Carolle grumbled. "I'm Carolle Graean, through and through. Always a river rat." She exhaled. "Suppose there's no real escaping who we are, is there?"

Gbad'Wu said, "That is a terrible thing to hope for. Whatever name you call yourself, whatever pieces you present, you are always you. There should be comfort in that."

Carolle let the comment go.

"Do better, be better," the monk said. "An old friend's words I repeat too often." She put her fingertips to Carolle's arm to gain her attention. "You will dance again, and when you do, may you never stop."

Dawn outlined the mountains across the bay when they reached the wharf for passenger vessels. A few piers already had passengers queueing.

"Gbad'Wu?"

"Oui?"

"There's something else I've done." The monk put her hand on her hip but listened without judgment in her expression. "I may have—no, I did. I did send an invitation to Ludmilla Leupp to attend a secret ball at the castle. With instructions to gain access by wearing a mask of King Vendral. Also provided by me."

Gbad'Wu tittered. "The queen mentioned another find this evening." The monk bit back her smile and shook her head. "You break more traditions than you are aware. May Veen forgive me for bringing you home. He will have his hands full with a pupil as stubborn as you."

"People don't say 'no' to you often, do they?" Carolle asked. Warned with a look, Carolle let the question go. "So what kind of traditions am I breaking now?"

"Par exemple," Gbad'Wu said, "I always bring two pupils to the Mount of Ukresti when I return. One who needs our help and one who can train and return to strengthen their community. It sets a balance. However, this is not an option with your troupe. I would weaken them more."

"Last call!" a husky dockworker called from the pier. "The Wave Bender sets sail now!"

Carolle slowed on the planks and stared at Gbad'Wu as she thought. "I am stubborn," she said, dropping her chin in surrender. She inhaled the sea air deeply and strode along the pier past the dockworker.

Gbad'Wu chased after her. "Where are you going?"

"We need to take the Wave Bender to Deganwy. Patevia isn't on our way, but you can find your pupil in my village." Carolle hesitated at the gangway but carried on with a nod to herself. "I should be there for my mam when she dies."

THANK YOU FOR READING!

IF YOU ENJOYED *GILT*, PLEASE WRITE A REVIEW. YOUR ENCOURAGING WORDS BRIGHTEN MY DAY AND INSPIRE ME TO CONTINUE SHARING MORE TALES FROM CYR.

Other Books in the Lamentation's End series:

About the Author

Wade Lewellyn-Hughes is an author, screenwriter, and general creative based in Montana. Aiming to bring a vivid world and robust characters to life, he values diversity and differences in this world and the one he's writing.

Sign up for updates on upcoming books and find out more here: http://wadelewellyn.com

.

www.ingramcontent.com/pod-product-compliance
Lightning Source LLC
Chambersburg PA
CBHW051955170626
46808CB00007B/2636